I0846696

CYNTHIA HICKEY

Cowboy Jeopardy

Cynthia Hickey

The Cowboys of Misty Hollow, Book 1

ISBN-13: 978-1-962168-40-3

To all those who love a cowboy!

Chapter One

Danica Cooper's legs trembled as she walked up the lane leading to the big house. Her suitcase thumped over the cracks behind her.

It had been three months since the fiasco with the Roberto family and her gambling addiction that had almost gotten her and her family killed. Still, she felt woefully inadequate to accept the job as girl Friday and nanny to ten-year-old twin boys. Was the father unaware of her past, or was he so desperate he'd hire anyone?

The folks of Misty Hollow, while friendly enough, still watched her with wary eyes despite adoring her twin sister, Delaney. But then, Delly had married one of the town's favorite deputies while Dani had gone to rehab.

Horses grazed in paddocks on each side of her, doing little to still the nervous flutters in her gut. What if her new boss, Dylan Wyatt, canned her the instant he found out? What would she do then? She couldn't work at the diner anymore. It got old being compared to her perfect sister all the time. Not to mention living with their mother in the camper. No, Dani needed a place of her own, and a chance to start a new life after being almost killed.

She squared her shoulders and pressed the doorbell. Westminster chimes rang out. She stepped back and licked dry lips.

The door swung open. A massive man with coal black hair and piercing blue eyes stared down at her before a slow smile curved chiseled lips. "Miss Cooper?"

"Yes, sir." This hunk must be her new boss. Yowza. She hadn't seen him…well, she had seen him. The cowboys had helped patrol the streets during her trouble, but she hadn't known which one was him.

"Wonderful. Come on in. I'll show you around while the boys, Eric and Derrick, are at school." He snatched her suitcase from the porch as if it didn't weigh more than five pounds, but which in actuality contained everything she owned. "Here is a photo of the rascals. One of your tasks will be taking them to school and picking them up. Of course, summer break is only a couple of weeks away. Let me show you to your room."

He led her across polished wood floors and up a wide staircase. "These two rooms belong to the boys and are connected by a Jack-and-Jill bathroom. You're right here across the hall." He pushed open a set of double doors.

Wow. A four-poster bed adorned with a colorful quilt took up the space between two windows. A door to her left revealed a bathroom. Another door opened into a closet. A carved armoire took up another wall.

"I hope it's sufficient."

"It's beautiful." Her few clothes wouldn't make a

dent in the closet, much less the armoire.

"Great. Let's start the tour. You don't really have a specific time to wake up, especially once summer starts, but the boys don't usually sleep much later than six or six-thirty. Once they go to bed at night, the hours are yours, and you have Sundays off."

Dani nodded, not minding the early hours. She'd be up before then anyway.

He showed her the kitchen where she'd help the cook, Mrs. White, with the meals when she wasn't busy with the boys. "She's not here right now, but basically, you'll help with whatever needs doing if the boys are at school." He flashed a grin, revealing a dimple in his right cheek. "Even work in the barn. During the summer, the boys have a list of chores. You'll make sure they do them." He didn't ask any questions; he simply rattled off her duties as they strolled the property.

Positioned on the top of Misty Mountain, few trees filled the acreage. Instead, red outbuildings and many horses provided a pleasant landscape. She'd heard that an extra-special forces vet had purchased and renovated the Rocking W Ranch, but hadn't seen the place. Impressive, to say the least.

"I'll introduce you to the men at lunch. They're a great group of guys. All ex-military needing a new start in life."

"Like me," she muttered. Minus the military.

"Exactly."

"So, you do know who I am?" She stopped and peered up at him. "I'd wondered."

"Because I didn't say anything?" He quirked a brow. "One of the things we value here, Miss Cooper, is discretion. As long as the work is done to my satisfaction, and trouble doesn't come knocking on my doorstep, I'm good with an employee who used to be in trouble. I trust you're no longer that person."

"I'm not." She felt more relaxed than she had since her ride had dropped her off at the entrance to the Rocking W.

"Then we'll get along fine. I mean it when I say this is a place for fresh beginnings. No one will judge you here, Miss Cooper, as long as you stay clean, do no harm, and do what is expected of you."

"Please, call me Dani. I can follow those expectations."

"Great. I'm Dylan."

Her phone dinged. She glanced at the text message.

Watch your back. This isn't over. You still have a debt to pay.
Not even a big cowboy can save you from your transgressions.

~

Dylan frowned at Dani's pale face. She took a deep shuddering breath and shoved her phone into the pocket of her jeans. "Everything all right?"

"Yes." She gave a shaky smile. "Wrong number."

His frown deepened. The flitter of fear across her features and the way she avoided eye contact let him know she had lied. He exhaled heavily and led the way to the barn. Had he made a mistake in hiring her? He hoped not. "Do you ride, Dani?"

She shook her head and stepped back as Lightning, his dapple-gray stallion, stuck his head over the stall door in greeting. "Never had the need."

"This is my pride and joy. He's used for stud and doesn't let anyone but me ride him." Dylan rubbed the horse's muzzle. "He won't bite you. It's important you learn to ride. My sons love to and ride every chance they get. You'll need to accompany them on occasion. I've just the horse for you to learn on."

"Lord have mercy," she whispered.

He chuckled. "Seriously, you'll be fine. Meet Daisy." He led her to a roan mare with a white blaze. "She's as gentle as a kitten."

"Kittens have claws and sharp teeth." She reached out a timid hand.

"Where's the brave woman who faced down a murderous loan shark?" Still grinning, he raised a brow.

A laugh escaped her. "Guess a horse is nothing in comparison. Thank you for your help in…keeping the town safe during all that."

"Hey, that's what cowboys do." He patted her shoulder. "We'll start your riding lesson this afternoon. Let's meet the rest of the crew, then you can help Mrs. White prepare lunch."

One cowboy led a horse in a circle around a paddock, another forked hay, and multiple others swarmed the yard. Poor Dani. She looked like a deer caught in the headlights as he rattled off their names.

"I'll never remember them all."

"Sure, you will. In time. You won't have much to do with them outside of mealtimes, but they're a good, if not quiet group. They won't give you any trouble." Heads would roll if they did. Dylan prided himself on being a fair boss, but he was also a stickler for the rules. Respect was the number-one rule. "That's the bunkhouse. It's off limits to the boys, so it's off limits to you."

"Not a problem. I'm here to do my job, nothing more." A determined look settled over her face. "I appreciate the opportunity you've given me for a new start and won't mess that up."

He certainly hoped not. There weren't many folks in Misty Hollow willing to take on his two boys. The fact Dani was a twin herself had worked in her favor. Hopefully, she had the strength to deal with rowdy boys with a mischievous streak ten miles long. The last nanny had run off without collecting her paycheck.

He eyed the petite woman at his side and stifled a sigh. The boys would trample her unless he put the fear of God in them. Something he planned on doing the moment they returned home from school.

When they entered the kitchen through the back door, Mrs. White turned with a smile. "I wondered when I'd get to meet the only other woman in this house."

"This is Dani Cooper. Dani, Mrs. White. You'll help her when she needs it, if—" He smiled at the older woman, "you aren't busy with the boys."

"Pshaw. I'll put those two rascals to work, too. It's good to meet you, Dani."

"Likewise. Is there anything I can help you with to prepare for lunch?" Dani reached for an apron on the wall.

Good. Dylan smiled and left the room. He liked the fact that she'd jump right in where needed. As for him, he had bookkeeping to tend to while the house was relatively quiet.

After his father had died two years ago, Dylan sold

the ranch in Texas and rebuilt it on Misty Mountain, preferring hills and hollows to flat land with no trees. It hadn't been easy, or cheap, but the renovated house had been worth it. If only Lauren had been alive to see the fruition of her dream. His wife had been an Arkansas born-and-bred girl. Coming here was his tribute to her and the legacy he promised to leave her sons.

What would she have thought of his giving people like his ranch hands and Dani a second chance? She would have agreed. His wife's heart had been filled with the desire to help others.

He flipped open the ledger on his desk, confirming he was about tapped out of funds. If he didn't get some foals to sell soon, he'd be up the proverbial creek without a paddle. Letting any of his hands go wasn't an option. Nor was letting the new nanny go. Hopefully, without having to focus on the boys, at least for now, he could come up with some ideas to make money fast.

He tapped a pencil on his desk blotter. Maybe tours for the elementary school? Guided campouts during the summer? Dylan had the options if he could find the time. He had several tame horses children could ride, and he could buy more if he needed to. It might benefit his boys to help out with these things.

Nodding, he glanced up as the cowbell rang for lunch. He glanced out the window to see Dani ringing it. Scratching the back of his neck, he pushed to his feet. The woman was one more expense. Dylan prayed she'd be worth the money.

Chapter Two

Dani pulled into the pickup line at the school. Dylan had told her the boys would recognize the truck and knew their new nanny would be coming for them. Hopefully, she'd get no trouble from them. If they were anything close to as ornery as she and Delly had been, she was in for a world of hurt.

The two boys emerged from the school and tussled with some other boys before stopping and glancing up and down the pickup line. One of them said something to the other, then they made their way at a snail's pace to the truck. Dani hoped she'd learn to tell them apart quickly.

Both boys stared silently through the window.

"Hey, I'm Dani. Get in." She smiled, thrusting the door open.

"We thought when Dad said Dani, we were getting a boy nanny." One of them frowned. "You're just another girl."

"Thanks for noticing. My full name is Danica, but I go by Dani. Come on."

After a quick glance at each other, they climbed in.

"Seatbelts." She arched a brow.

"Dad doesn't make us wear them."

"I doubt that." She tilted her head and gave them her best "I-won't-take-any-nonsense look"—something her mother had given her a million times while growing up.

They scowled and clicked their seatbelts into place.

"So, who is who?" She pulled away from the curb.

"I'm Eric, and he's Derrick."

Which meant the opposite. She stamped their features into her mind. Eric had a cowlick on the crown of his head. Derrick's left eyebrow arched a tiny bit more than his brother's. She smiled. It was enough to know who was who.

"What are you grinning at?" Eric crossed his arms. "No one said anything funny."

"I'm thinking of all the fun we're going to have."

"Yeah, like what?" Derrick tilted his head.

"Well, after your homework is done, I thought I'd let you two give me a tour of the grounds. Your father and I were a bit rushed during the tour earlier."

"You scared of the woods?"

"No, why?" She shot them a quick glance.

"Sasquatch. One of our classmates said she saw one once."

Derrick elbowed his brother. "That turned out to be a killer, dummy."

"Did not!" The two wrestled, bumping Dani's arm.

The truck veered into the opposite lane. She steered it back where it belonged. "Not in the truck, boys." Her harsh tone snapped them to attention. "We can go bigfoot hunting if you want, but only after your homework is done."

"We don't have any," Eric said.

"Yes, you do. I emailed your teacher." She hadn't,

not yet anyway, but she intended to on a daily basis. Yes, being a twin herself definitely worked in her favor.

Her mother had almost bust a gut laughing when Dani told her about the job. She called it payback. Maybe so.

"There you go grinning again." Eric scowled. "You stay in your head a lot, don't you? Must be hilarious in there."

A laugh escaped her. Maybe this job would be more fun than not.

After a snack of still-warm chocolate chip cookies and milk, the two boys settled down at the kitchen table to do their homework while Dani helped Mrs. White with supper preparations. "When they're finished, they want to go into the woods at the back of the property. Do you think their father will mind?"

"Not if an adult is with them. They go out that way a lot."

"We'll take Monster."

Dani shot a look over her shoulder. "Who is Monster?"

"Their brute of a dog," the chef answered. "Mean-looking, but very sweet. Usually, he's waiting at the road for the…ah, there he is." She opened the back door to let in the biggest, muddiest dog Dani had ever seen.

"Fitting name."

The dog sat and tenderly took a cookie offered by Mrs. White. "Cupcake would be a more fitting name." She grinned and patted the dog's neck. "I see why he wasn't here. He's been in the creek. Monster loves the water. I hope you like dogs because he's the third twin most of the time."

"If she doesn't—" Derrick said looking up, "then

we can't be friends." He returned his attention to his homework.

"Good thing I like dogs, then." She stifled a laugh and started chopping onions.

"Dad!"

She turned as the boys raced to their father and wrapped their arms around his waist. "Good afternoon."

"Ladies." He nodded and ruffled his sons' hair. "Sorry, I didn't join you for the snack, boys. I was neck deep in the ledger."

"You hate the ledger," Eric muttered. "It makes you grouchy."

"Not all the time." He shrugged Dani's way. "Anyway, boys, I have something I'd like to discuss with you if you have the time."

"Sure, Dad. We can take a break." Eric said, then they returned to the table and closed their notebooks.

"Does he always treat them like little men?" She whispered to Mrs. White.

"When they're not misbehaving. He has ever since their momma died two years ago. Horse-riding accident."

Her blood rushed to her toes. "I'm supposed to learn how to ride tomorrow."

"Don't worry." She clapped a flour-covered hand on Dani's shoulder. "Accidents are rare."

"What's your idea, Dad?"

"This concerns the women, too. Mind if we include them in this discussion?"

Dani turned as the boys nodded. At the urging of Mrs. White, she sat next to Derrick on the bench seat of the small kitchen table.

"My ideas to bring in some funds until we have

foals ready to sell will increase everyone's workload." Dylan reached for a cookie. "But, it should be heaps of fun, too."

"Spill the beans." Mrs. White planted fists on her rounded hips. "I don't have all day."

He laughed, then choked and reached for Derrick's unfinished milk. After holding up a finger for them to wait, he took a few swallows, then cleared his throat. "Okay, Mrs. Impatient. I'm thinking about opening up the ranch to tours from the school, day camps, summer camps, and overnight guided camping. Horseback lessons, that sort of stuff." He grinned.

Dani widened her eyes. "How does this affect me?" Her responsibility lay with the boys.

"I'm going to need the help of my sons. They're avid riders and know these woods. The boys can be an inspiration to the other kids and can actually lead some of the lessons."

Mrs. White sighed. "I'll ask my niece to come help me clean those rooms in that empty bunkhouse. I reckon you plan on putting that to use."

"For youth groups, yes." He pushed to his feet. "I'm going to start on advertising. I'd like to have this up and running when school is out, and I need to tell the guys."

"Good ideas, Dad. We're going big-foot hunting in a while." Eric opened his notebook. "It'll be a big hit with the tours!"

Dylan glanced at Dani. "Big foot?"

"The boys' idea." She shrugged. "I'd like to get to know the woods around here anyway."

"Good idea. Take Monster with you." He patted the dog's head and left the room.

~

Big foot. Dylan chuckled and grabbed his black Stetson from the hook near the front door. *What will my boys think of next?* Knowing the men would be wrapping up for the day, he rang the bell next to the barn. They'd all gather within fifteen minutes.

How would they take the news? With some grumbling, most likely. Most of them had come to the Rocking W for peace and solitude. But, if he were to keep them on the payroll, he needed a way to pay them.

Dylan leaned against the barn, leg bent and boot flat against the wall behind him. The screen door to the kitchen banged as his boys barged out, Monster on their heels. Some would say that a house as grand as his didn't need a back screen door, but he liked the sound of it. Lauren would've loved it, and it let him know when someone left or entered.

Dani followed close on the boys' heels, stopping the door from banging behind her, then hopped off the deck and took off at a sprint after the rascals. This was the main reason he hadn't hired an older, more inexperienced nanny. They would never have been able to keep up.

Colt Dawson was the first hand to arrive. "Trouble, Boss?"

"No, changes." Dylan tipped his hat further on his head. "More work for everyone."

"No one will mind. We're grateful to be here."

"You might mind this. It involves women and children. Possibly lots of children."

"Heaven forbid." Colt laughed. "Again, no one will mind. We'll do whatever it takes to help." He narrowed his eyes. "You left the ledger open the other day. I snuck a peek. Sorry."

Dylan quirked his mouth. "As foreman, you have a right to know. We'll be fine next year, but we need funds now."

He nodded. "Can't wait to hear what you're thinking."

Hopefully, he wouldn't change his mind after hearing his plan. One by one the others gathered in front of him. Dylan met each of their gazes, then repeated what he'd told the women. "We have two weeks to get ready. Any objections?"

"Who's going to take care of the livestock?" His hand, Maverick, asked.

"We are, same as now. The only change will be that during the camps, the campers will help out. It's part of the package, the experience."

"So, we'll be slowed down by folks who don't know a lick about what they're doing?"

"Yep, that pretty much sums it up."

Maverick took a deep breath, then released it slowly. "Okay."

"That's it?" Dylan glanced around the group. "No objections? No more questions?"

"No, sir." Ryder shook his head. "We trust you. If you feel the need to do this, then we're all for it. I do have one concern, though."

"What is it?"

"Opening up the ranch lets in all types of characters. Not all of them will have good intentions. Have you thought about the boys? The women?"

"I have. Dani Cooper has been in the midst of hell, same as we have, only...different. She'll have good instincts about trouble." *God, please let me be right.*

"What do you want us to do now?" Colt tugged his hat firmly on his head.

"I'll post duties by morning." He cleared his throat, emotion surging at how willing these men were to help him. "I thank every one of you."

"It's us who thank you." Colt nodded and marched off as the others peeled away to finish their tasks before supper.

Dylan glanced to where Dani and the boys had gone, tempted to follow, but he shrugged off the idea. He had a lot to do in the next couple of weeks. Pricing, advertising, getting the remaining outbuildings in shape. Work that would lie on his shoulders. His men were already working the maximum number of hours.

His boots kicked up dust as he headed for the storage shed. The area hadn't seen rain in weeks, but the forecast predicted that would change. The empty bunkhouse roof needed patching before then. Once that danger was past, he'd check each room on the inside.

What about families? The overnight camping trips would be open to both children and accompanying adults. Day and week camps would be for youth ten to eighteen-years-old. Great. Dylan had added a monumental task to his list. He needed places for families to stay.

He eyed the main house. There was space in the turrets. It would be the simplest fix, and he could have stairs built leading to them from the outside in order to keep the guests out of the main house. It could work. As funds allowed, he'd expand.

Grinning, he opened the door to the storage building and grabbed the ladder. He'd placed shingles on the roof of the building needing repairs weeks ago.

Now, he had a couple of hours to devote to the task. Dylan propped the ladder against the building and climbed to where he'd left supplies. The whole roof could stand to be replaced, but patching would have to do for the time being. He laid out some shingles and grabbed the nail gun.

A scream rang out from the woods.

He whipped around at the sound. His boot slipped from where he stood on the slope of the roof, and he slid toward its edge.

Chapter Three

Dylan's shirt rode up as he slid down the roof, exposing his ribcage to the rough shingles. Fire burned as he left flesh behind. He yelled and grabbed for the gutter, stopping his fall. His legs flailed as he tried to find the ladder.

"Whoa, Boss." Colt held the ladder still. "Want me to fix you a harness?"

"No, I do not." Dylan glared and moved to the ladder. "I lost my footing is all. Thought I heard someone scream."

"You did. Eric splashed his brother with cold creek water." Colt grinned up at him, then sobered just as quickly. "You expecting trouble with the new nanny being here?"

"They won't find Bigfoot with that noise." Dylan climbed back to the roof.

"What?"

"Nothing. No, I'm not expecting trouble." He hoped. "Thanks for coming to my rescue."

"No problem. It wasn't but a few feet to the ground. You'd have been fine. I'll help you with the inside when I've finished my other job." Gravel crunched as the other man sauntered away.

Dylan needed to keep his head in the game, or there would be medical expenses to pay on top of everything else. No more screams or shouts of alarm came from the woods to distract him. Nothing to keep him from the job at hand except his thoughts. Thoughts that settled on the blond woman he'd hired to watch his boys.

Were the men wary of her? Her former gambling debts had created a lot of trouble for the town of Misty Hollow. People had died, including the loan shark who had followed her to town. That was all behind her, right? The Rocking W was a place of second chances. That pertained to those not only with PTSD, but also with addictions. Who was he to turn away one person over another? A concerned father, that's who. One with a niggling at the edge of his mind that wouldn't go away.

Dylan glanced toward the woods. Dani and the boys should be heading back this way soon for supper. He could relax then.

~

"Boys, stop." Dylan would have a fit when he saw his sopping wet boys. "Let's get out of the water and continue the hunt. We'll have to head back soon for supper." Dani needed to help Mrs. White. Feeding all the hands was too much work for one person.

"Okay." Eric splashed his brother one more time, then climbed from the creek. "We need to find some footprints."

Dani heaved a sigh. Finally, the boys were back on the original track of finding the fabled creature. "If we follow the creek, we might see evidence in the mud."

"Bigfoot is too smart for that." Derrick shot her a

look that clearly said she wasn't too bright. "He'll be sneakier. Nothing keeps Bigfoot from being caught this long by being stupid."

And yet the two ten-year-olds thought they could outsmart such a creature, not that Bigfoot actually existed. "Half an hour more, no longer." She doubted they paid her any attention.

The boys scrambled along the creek, heads down, stopping occasionally to study a scuff. After determining it wasn't a footprint, they moved on.

Late afternoon shadows deepened. "We should really think about heading back, boys."

"In a minute. We found something."

Dani joined them near a boulder. A clear footprint showed in the damp soil. "That's a gym shoe, guys, not an animal print."

"Maybe Bigfoot wears shoes now." Eric glanced up.

"His feet would be much bigger than that. It's most likely one of the cowboys."

"They all wear boots." Derrick shook his head. "It's a mystery, Dani. One we need to solve."

"We're moving on from finding Bigfoot?" *Thank you, God.*

He nodded. "Dad doesn't allow people back here. Since we haven't started those dumb tours, this is a trespasser."

Her mouth dried up, and she glanced around the darkening woods. "Let's head back."

"Five more minutes."

"No, I'm the adult here, and we're going back right now." She added as much sternness to her voice as possible. These two needed to know when she meant business. "I have to help Mrs. White if anyone wants to eat supper. I think we're having fried chicken."

"Yippee!" Footprint forgotten, Derrick straightened. "My favorite. Come on, Eric. If we're late, all the legs will be gone."

Dani turned, then stopped. Everything suddenly looked the same. Except for the creek. Follow the creek back to where the boys had played, then turn...left. "Where's Monster?"

"He doesn't like to get wet," Eric said. "Ran off when we started splashing. He'll be back." The boy frowned. "What's wrong?"

"We might be lost."

"No, we aren't." He marched ahead of her. "Don't be silly. Follow me."

After several minutes, they stopped. "Is there where you played in the water?" Dani studied the area. Any splashed water had dried.

Something crashed in the bushes next to her. She whirled and gasped.

Monster darted from the foliage, tongue lolling.

"You crazy dog. How about you show us the way home?" She patted his head. "Obviously, none of us are certain." How could she have let them get lost?

"We aren't lost." Eric glared. "We played right over there. You sat on that log. What's wrong with you?" He turned left and continued.

"We play in here all the time," Derrick said, following his brother. "You'll get used to things."

Not fast enough. She made a mental note of landmarks as she moved through the trees. Ahead, she spotted the clearing where the afternoon shadows had yet to darken.

A twig snapped behind her.

She put a hand to her throat. "Monster, you need to stop scaring me." She gave a nervous laugh and turned.

Something moved between the trees. Something on two legs.

Monster moved to her side. His hackles rose, and a deep growl vibrated from his throat.

"Easy, boy." Dani backed up. Instinct told her it was not a friendly person flitting from shadow to shadow. If it was one of the cowboys, they'd have called out a greeting. She whipped around to face the clearing.

The house rose in the distance. "Last one to the house helps with dishes." She ushered the boys to move faster.

Breath rasping in her lungs, Dani burst through the back door of the kitchen.

"Mercy." Mrs. White spun, flinging mashed potatoes from a wooden spoon and onto the floor. "Are you being chased by a bear? Look what you made me do."

"A race." Eric grinned.

"Go wash up while Dani helps me." She shook her head. When they were gone, she turned to Dani, grabbing a rag as she did. "Something spook you?"

"I'm sure it was nothing, except for the crazy feeling of being lost." She pulled an apron from a nearby hook, then washed her hands. "Silly, really. The boys knew the way the whole time."

"Of course, they did." She frowned, cleaned up the spatters on the floor, then turned back to mashing the potatoes. "Give that gravy a stir, would you? And help me keep an eye on the biscuits. I expected you back earlier."

"I'm sorry." Dani glanced at the clock. "When do you need me back each day?"

"By four."

Ouch. She was more than an hour late. Any excursions with the boys would have to be on the weekends and days they had no school. "I won't be late again."

The older woman laughed. "Yes, you will. Those boys will monopolize your time. You watch and see."

Dani grinned. "Okay, but I promise to do my best."

"That's all any of us can do. After supper, I suggest you tell Dylan what spooked you out there. Man or animal needs to be taken care of."

"Nothing much gets past you, does it?"

"Nope."

Supper was loud and rowdy with the cowboys ribbing each other, the boys laughing and shouting to be heard. Dani hadn't ever had a meal as much fun that she could remember outside of family holidays. Maybe she could invite her mother… "My mother would probably love to help with the preparations for the upcoming camps." She glanced at Dylan.

"I don't have the funds to pay her right now." His face darkened.

"She's bored out of her mind. I'm sure she'll like staying busy."

"We can use her." Mrs. White put another bowl of biscuits on the table. "Didn't you say she lives in a camper? There's room to park it next to the barn. That would give her some privacy."

Dylan chuckled, the embarrassed flush gone from his face. "If she's willing, then I'll be glad to have all the help I can get. I can't pay her for a while. Make sure she understands that."

"Plus, she can help in the kitchen, freeing Dani up to be with the boys more." Mrs. White gave a definitive nod as if the matter was settled. "Now, Dani has something to tell you about the excursion into the woods."

Dani shot her a shocked look. "You said after supper."

"Might as well do it while the men are all here. More eyes to keep a lookout."

"Did you see Bigfoot?" Dylan winked.

She glanced at the curious expressions on the twins' faces. "No, but I did spot someone on two legs. Someone who didn't want to be seen."

He set his fork on the edge of his plate. "Doing what?"

"Staying to the shadows mostly. I had the definite impression he—I'm pretty sure it was a man who was watching me and the boys." Had trouble followed her? Her mind flitted back to the warning she'd received via text. If it had, she'd have to leave. She wouldn't put the children in danger.

"Maverick, you and Rider take a look after supper. See what you can find out."

"We saw footprints by the creek." Eric waved his biscuit. "We wanted to solve the mystery of who left them. Us, Dad. Not the cowboys."

Dylan narrowed his eyes. "Until the mystery is solved, the two of you are to stay out of the woods."

~

It wasn't going to be easy getting close to the woman on a ranch full of armed cowboys. He exhaled heavily. The boss wasn't going to be happy to hear that bit of news. The task assigned was to grab the woman and make her face the trouble she'd caused. Hang the boss. He planned on getting the money for himself.

With one last glance toward the main house, he turned back into the woods and turned on his headlamp. He'd have to find a way to blend in until he could get close enough to her. Not easy in a town where everyone knew everyone else. A newcomer stuck out like a green Martian.

He headed to the campground and the camper he'd rented for an indeterminate amount of time. Better than a tent or a motel room, but he was used to more luxurious accommodations. Having worked for the Roberto family for over ten years and having been secretly involved in an affair with the daughter, he'd had everything he ever wanted. Until now. He hadn't pretended to love the plain, bossy daughter of Roberto for nothing.

All that had been taken away from him by one blond-haired woman who owed a lot of money to the Roberto family. Money he intended to get his hands on, one way or the other.

Chapter Four

Dani's mother narrowed her eyes over the rim of her coffee cup. "You want me to go help you with your job in order to not have to pay rent on this campsite? Am I hearing you right? You really expect me to deal with twins, after you and your sister, for no pay? Not to mention cowboys and a horde of other children come summer break?"

"It doesn't sound very appealing when you put it that way." Dani slid from the booth in the dining nook of the camper. "Sorry I bothered you."

"Hold on. I didn't say I wouldn't do it." She took a sip before setting her cup down. "I've gotten a bit bored and lonely with you and Delly off living your own lives. It wouldn't hurt for me to be around another woman my age for a while." She winked. "And there's never been anything wrong with being surrounded by cowboys."

"Oh." Dani laughed. "None of them are your age, but they are all very good-looking."

"That'll be just fine. You tell that Rancher Wyatt I'll be there by the end of the day."

"You don't need to for two weeks."

"I might as well get settled in."

"Okay. I'm off to learn how to ride a horse." A tremor of fear slithered down her spine.

"Think of the horse as a big dog. One you ride and will most likely fall off of." Her mother grinned.

"Gee, thanks." Dani gave her mom a quick hug, then headed to the truck Dylan had assigned for her to use.

Half an hour later, she hurried into the kitchen to let Mrs. White know that her mother would be arriving that afternoon. "She says she wants to be here early enough to be prepared."

"Wonderful. That will free up some of your time. You'll be crazy busy once school is out." She handed Dani a dish towel. "Dylan said to meet him at the paddock at ten."

Dani glanced at the clock. She had an hour to work on her nerves, which wasn't long enough. By the end of the hour, her hands shook. She'd done nothing but think of "what ifs" while drying dishes and cleaning the kitchen.

With a few minutes to spare, she trudged toward the paddock where Dylan stood with the roan mare he planned on her riding. She took a deep breath and opened the gate.

His eyes sparkled as he glanced over. "It isn't the guillotine, Dani. You might find out you love riding once you've learned how."

"Don't hold your breath."

The horse's ears twitched as his laugh rang out. "Come give Daisy a pet and a sugar cube. She'll be your best friend."

She took a deep shuddering breath and stretched her hand out.

Dylan put his larger one around hers and pulled her closer. "Right here. Her muzzle is as soft as velvet."

Dani closed her eyes and stroked the mare. "It is soft."

"I wouldn't lie to you. Come on." Keeping hold of her hand, he led her to a sawed-off stump. "From here, you'll put your left foot in the stirrup, then swing your right up and over the saddle."

"Are you crazy?" She frowned. "I'm way too short."

"No, you're not. I'll help you until you can do it yourself. If the boys can, you can."

Lord, help me. Dani climbed onto the stump.

"Grip the saddle horn."

"The what?" She stared down at him.

"That curved thing at the front of the saddle. Then, left foot in the stirrup. It's hanging down the side."

That she did know. With a deep breath, she tried following his instructions…and failed.

"Here you go." He reached for her as she slid down.

His hands cupped around her rear and hoisted her up.

Her breath escaped her. "Oh."

"Sorry."

He didn't sound sorry. In fact, he sounded amused. She heard a definite laugh in his voice. Dani glared at him as she settled into the saddle.

"Really, it wasn't intended." A dimple winked in his cheek.

Maybe not, but his touch had sent a bolt of electricity through her she had no business feeling. The man was her boss, nothing more. She gripped the reins.

"Now what?"

"Loosen your grip, or you'll hurt Daisy's mouth. She only needs gentle guidance." He took the reins from her. "Hold onto the saddle horn. I'll lead you in a circle until you get a feel for her movement." He led the horse at a slow pace.

Dani tried concentrating on the rhythm, but her gaze kept landing on the muscles rippling through his tee-shirt. She was acting like a silly teenager over an accidental touch. If it hadn't affected him, it shouldn't mean anything to her.

"How ya doin'?"

"Fine."

"Good." He turned and handed her the reins. "Pull right to go right, pull left to go left, pull back to stop, gentle kick to go. All your movements should be gentle. Don't hurt my old girl." He stepped back and motioned for her to circle the paddock.

It seemed simple enough. She could do this. Dani gave a soft kick.

The horse moved forward, then stopped at the paddock railing.

"You need to turn her," Dylan called out.

"Right." She tugged.

The horse neighed and jerked its head.

"Too harsh. Be gentle." Dylan moved forward and patted Daisy's neck. "She won't respond well to a rough hand. Think of her as a woman, same as you. A gentle touch always works best."

She started to give a smart-aleck remark about a man knowing what a woman wanted, but then remembered he'd been married. She gave a softer pull on the rein and grinned as Daisy turned. "She did it."

"Daisy needs very little encouragement." He leaned against the railing and crossed his arms.

She could feel the heat of his stare as she rode around the paddock. After the fifth time, he said they'd had enough. Shortly after, the cowbell rang across the property, signaling lunchtime.

Dani slid from the saddle. Her legs buckled under her.

"Whoa." Dylan rushed forward and caught her. "That happens to newbies."

"Thanks." She glanced up, her gaze clashing with his.

~

Wide eyes the color of prairie grass peered up at him. His breath hitched. He steadied her and stepped back as if she were a snake ready to strike.

When he'd helped her into the saddle, his hands being more intimate than he'd intended, he'd stifled a laugh. But this…the closeness…stole his breath. He cleared his throat. "You did good. Real good for your first time."

"Thank you." She ducked her head and turned as a camper pulled up to the house. "Oh. My mother is here."

Spotting Colt and Maverick emerging from the woods, he nodded. "I'll come meet her in a bit."

"Okay." She headed to greet her mother while he marched toward his men.

"Anything?" He searched their faces.

"Definitely footprints not belonging to any of us." Colt showed him a photo on his phone. "Gym shoes, not boots."

"A lost hiker?"

"Maybe, but we spotted the tracks by the creek in several places." Colt's eyes hardened. "It appeared as if this person was following Dani and the boys. Then, he stopped at the edge of the trees, probably looking toward the house, long enough for his prints to be deeper there than in other places."

"Definitely watching the house, Boss." Maverick nodded.

Dylan drew a breath sharply through his nose. It appeared as if trouble had followed Dani to the Rocking W. "We'll need to set up a guard schedule, but don't make it look like what it is. I don't want the women or children to worry. Especially with our camp opening soon."

The timing of trouble couldn't be worse.

"We got you." Maverick tugged his hat firmly on his head. "We'll pull on our military experience. The ranch couldn't be safer."

Dylan counted on it. He cast another glance toward the trees then turned for the house. "Lunchtime. You know how Mrs. White is when we're late."

Colt chuckled. "That's why we came back. I'm terrified of the woman, and I hear there's going to be another in the kitchen."

"Maybe Mrs. Cooper won't be as tough." Dylan grinned. "But, I heard stories during the time the Robertos were in town. From what I heard, she's tougher than any special-forces veteran. Kept Sheriff Westbrook on his toes."

"Good. If trouble is coming, we'll need her." Colt laughed.

Dylan wanted to laugh along with the others, but worry over the unknown threat made it impossible. He entered the main house through the back door and headed for the bathroom. After a quick washup, he joined the others in the dining room.

"Dylan, this is my mother, Marilyn Cooper." Dani carried a plate of hot biscuits to the table, still moving gingerly. She'd get used to horseback riding in time.

"Pleased to meet you, ma'am." He nodded.

"Marilyn, please." She planted fists on her hips, her eyes traveling around the room. "This all of you?"

"Except for my boys who are at school." He took his seat at the front of the table. He reached for a chicken leg from the plate being passed, then took another as the delicious aroma wafted to his nose. "Smells great."

"I make a mean fried chicken." Marilyn grinned and poured him a cup of coffee. "Don't tell me you don't drink coffee at noon. Cowboys drink it twenty-four seven is what I heard."

Dani's brows disappeared into her hairline. "Mom!"

"Well." Marilyn shrugged. "I'm right, aren't I?"

Dylan laughed. "Yes, ma'am, you're right." The woman was a hoot.

"I'm guessing my primary job here is to help Lenora, but I want you to know that I'll do whatever you need me to. Except lead guided tours with children. My naughty daughters were enough, thank you." She moved to fill other mugs with coffee.

"That's what I'm here for." Dani shook her head and set plates of butter on the table. "We weren't that bad."

Marilyn narrowed her eyes. "Need I remind you of the short time you've been out of rehab?"

"No." High spots of color appeared on Dani's cheeks.

"We don't bring up the past here, ma'am." Dylan would put an end to that right off. "There isn't one of us here who doesn't have a past. We embrace our pasts. They made us who we are today."

Rather than look chastised, she smiled. "Good. This is the perfect place for my girl. She can heal here."

"For crying out loud." Dani fell into a chair. "I'm starting to think it was a big mistake to bring you here."

The cowboys who had been watching the proceedings with amusement, broke into laughter.

"She's going to fit right in." Colt spooned mashed potatoes onto his plate.

Dylan agreed. Colorful characters were welcome on his ranch. He glanced out the large dining-room window. Just not the kind that brought trouble.

~

He stared at the advertisement taped to the window of the diner. Day camps for kids? Guided-camping trips? Riding lessons and survival-skill classes?

He hated the outdoors but here was a possible way for him to get onto the ranch without raising suspicion. Dani wouldn't expect a thing, and not having ever seen him, she wouldn't know that a snake hid in the grass.

A deadly one ready to strike.

Chapter Five

Dani's phone dinged the same time as the oven. She glanced at the oven timer, then pulled the cinnamon rolls from the oven before taking a peek at her phone screen. Her hands shook as she set the tray on the stovetop before glancing around to make sure she was alone. Her mother and Mrs. White were making up beds in preparation for the night when folks would be staying over before heading to the woods to camp. All students in Eric and Derrick's class had signed up for the first day of day camp. Thus, the need for cinnamon rolls for tomorrow's breakfast.

With a trembling hand, she read the third text warning of the day, and the clock had just turned seven a.m.

I'll be close, but you won't see me.

Then, we have some unfinished business, you and I.

I want my money.

Why wouldn't the sender simply come forward? Why play this stupid game? Whose money? The Roberto family were either dead or behind bars. Their money now belonged to the state of New York.

She sagged into a chair. The threats had slowed for a bit. There'd been no more sightings of strangers in the woods since that night. Why had the warnings started again this morning?

"What's wrong?"

She snapped up her head and stared at Dylan standing rigid in the kitchen doorway. "Nothing."

"Don't lie to me." He marched to the table and held out his hand. "May I see your phone please? This isn't the first time you've received something that made you look like a sheet of copy paper."

She thought about refusing. After all, her phone was her private business, but she was tired of carrying the burden of fear alone. Heaving a sigh, she dropped the device into his palm. "There's no log-in required."

The corner of his mouth quirked. "You might want to change that now that the boys are out of school. They like to take…interesting photos of the inside of their mouth and nose." His face grew grave as he read the text. "How many of these have you received?"

"One on the day I arrived and three today." She pushed to her feet and returned to work on the cinnamon rolls.

"Leave those. We're heading into town to talk to Sheriff Westbrook."

"That man hates me." Her shoulders sagged. Because of her, the sheriff's town had been thrust into danger and murder.

"The sheriff's a professional. He doesn't take crime personal."

"You haven't brought him any trouble." Quite the opposite. Dylan and his men had helped regain control of Misty Hollow after she'd brought a loan shark and his small army to town.

"Regardless, we're going." He tilted his head. "Or

should I have Marilyn nag you?"

"Heaven forbid." Dani saw no reason to involve her mother at this point. She'd only increase the stress level by a hundred percent. "Let me grab my purse."

She hurried to her room, brushed the flour off her face and shirt, smoothed her hair, then grabbed her purse from the nightstand drawer. No matter what Dylan said, the sheriff didn't care much for her. The man's stern gaze could pierce a wild boar, so she needed to look in control. "I'm ready." She joined Dylan at the front door.

"You look like you're expecting the guillotine." He opened the door and waved her through.

"I very well might be."

He grinned. "I never took you for such a dramatic person."

"Not dramatic. Realistic." She climbed into the truck before he could open the door for her. They weren't on a date. He was her boss and taking her somewhere she didn't really want to go.

Seatbelt clicked into place, she settled in for the ride down the mountain.

After a few minutes, Dylan cut her a quick glance. "You're awfully quiet."

"Just thinking. The sheriff is going to have a lot of questions, and I don't have any answers."

"He's going to wonder why you didn't come to him right away. Same as I'm wondering. After your recent trouble, it doesn't make a lot of sense."

Maybe not to him, but that first text has sent ice water through Dani's veins. Unfortunately, she was the type of person who usually ran and hid from trouble. This time she'd chosen to stay put and hope it all went away. Look how that had worked out for her. She sighed and leaned her head back. Mom was going to have a fit when she found out. "I guess I could've called my sister. She did marry a deputy, after all."

"He would've told you the same thing I did. Go to the sheriff."

"Which we're doing." She folded her hands tight enough in her lap to turn her knuckles white, and she worked on putting her mind in the right place to be interrogated.

When they arrived at the red-brick building which housed the sheriff's office, she thrust the truck door open and strode toward the buildings doors without waiting for Dylan. With his long legs, it didn't take him long to catch up and reach around her to open the door.

"Do you want me to go with you? For moral support?"

"Sure." She needed all the help she could muster.

The receptionist motioned for them to have a seat while she finished her phone call, then smiled at Dylan. "Mr. Wyatt, how may I help you?"

~

"We'd like to speak to the sheriff, please."

"One moment." She pressed a button on her phone, spoke into the receiver, then smiled. "Go on back. He's free."

The walk to the sheriff's office seemed a lot like a walk to the electric chair. She glanced at the floor to see whether someone had painted the tiles green.

"Relax." Dylan's soft touch on the small of her back didn't calm her. Instead, it sent her emotions whirling like a twister.

At Dylan's knock, the sheriff bade them enter. His

sharp gaze focused on Dani. "Miss Cooper."

"Sheriff." Her voice trembled as she took a seat across from him. The vinyl chair squeezed under her and released a soft whoosh of air.

"Dylan." Sheriff Westbrook stood and offered a handshake. "How can I help the two of you?"

Dylan sat next to Dani. "We have some impending trouble, I fear." He set Dani's phone on the sheriff's desk. "Dani has received some worrisome texts." He pulled them up on the screen.

The sheriff scrolled through them, a line forming between his eyes. When he finished, he copied and pasted the texts into a text to himself, then met their gazes. "Any idea who is sending these?"

"No, sir." Dani folded her hands in her lap.

"Roberto family?"

"As far as I know, they are all dead or behind bars."

Which didn't mean anything. There were ways of communicating from the inside. Dylan shook his head. "The ranch opens for camps and tours tomorrow, Sheriff."

He nodded. "Which means one of your guests could be the one sending these."

"Possibly. We have our first guided camp tour in two weeks, which will include adults. Tomorrow, we have people coming to see what we're all about, along with a group of school kids." Dread rose. "I'll be putting my men on guard, but we can't be everywhere at once."

"I might be able to spare someone to act as a ranch hand for a while. He'll be trained to spot something you or your men might miss." The sheriff crossed his arms and turned his attention back to Dani. "I advise you not to go anywhere alone, Miss Cooper. At least for the time being."

"I'm never alone. It's much worse than that, Sheriff. I always have the twins with me when they're not at school."

Dylan's heart skipped a beat. "They'll be staying close to the house until we find whoever is sending these texts." If he could, he'd lock the boys in the house. If he did though, they'd sneak out anyway. By giving them some freedom, he'd have a better chance of knowing where they were at all times.

"I'll have someone there this afternoon. Do you need anything else?"

Dani shook her head. "My mother is helping on the ranch."

The sheriff laughed. "God help whoever is threatening you. I wouldn't want to be on the wrong side of Marilyn Cooper. I came close enough a few months ago."

Dylan stood. "Thank you. We'll let you know if anything pops up."

"Thank you, Sheriff." Dani sprang to her feet and left the office ahead of Dylan.

In the hallway, he again put his hand on the small of her back. The warmth of her skin seeped through her shirt. "How about some lunch at the diner? Maybe some shopping after lunch until school is out. The boys get out early today, since it's the last day."

"I doubt I can eat anything, but okay, and I am running low on a few toiletries."

Rather than drive, they crossed the street and walked the short distance to the diner.

"Good afternoon." Lucy greeted them. "Want me to send Delly out?"

"Sure." It surprised him that Dani's twin continued working after getting married. He thought she'd be busy housekeeping. Maybe that would come after the babies. He gave his old-fashioned ideas a mental shake and followed Lucy to a booth.

"Hey, you two." Deputy Joey Hudson, Dani's new brother-in-law, glanced up from where he sat.

"Hey, to you."

"Join me." He motioned to the bench across from him. "I haven't eaten yet."

After a quick glance at Delly, who nodded, Dylan agreed. "We'd be glad to."

Delly approached them almost instantly. "I didn't know you were coming to town today." She smiled.

"Paid a visit to the sheriff," Dani mumbled.

"Why?" She paled.

Dylan filled her and her husband in on the texts.

"What does Mom say?"

Dani shrugged. "I haven't told her yet. I will later today, so don't go tattling. She's working at the ranch for a while."

"Oh, Sis. Why are you always in trouble?" Her eyes shimmered.

"This isn't new trouble. It's part of the old. At least that's what it sounds like."

"Your sister didn't ask for this." Dylan couldn't help coming to her rescue. The poor woman looked like a rejected kitten sitting there with slumped shoulders.

Delly shot him a sharp glance. "Trouble at the ranch and you with two young boys." The shimmers in her eyes had disappeared, replaced with a hard glint.

"That can't make you happy."

"It doesn't, but we'll weather whatever comes. I'll have the lunch special and coffee, please." He set his jaw, hoping she'd get the hint that the subject was closed.

"What does Sheriff Westbrook say?" Joey glanced from his wife to Dylan.

"He's going to send someone to stay on the ranch for a while. We have a lot of events coming up."

"I'll come hang out on my days off if Delly is working. We've handled plenty of threats in the past, and we can handle this one, too."

Dylan nodded. He sure hoped so. For the sake of his boys.

Chapter Six

Dani remained quiet on the drive from the school to the ranch, content to let the boys chatter on about their last day of school and their summer plans. Her mind stayed too full of worry. Several times, she considered putting in her notice and leaving the ranch. Dylan and his sons would be safer if she weren't there.

Trouble flocked after her like vultures to a fresh kill. There was no reason for anyone else to be in danger because of her.

The instant the boys slid from the truck, Dylan turned to her. "Forget it."

"What?" She reached for the door handle.

"Forget leaving. You're safer here than out there alone."

"But…"

"End of subject. I'll only haul your butt back." He shoved his door open. "You've got men with guns here…not to mention your mother." He smiled.

She tried to return the smile but failed. "It would be best for everyone if I were alone."

"No, it wouldn't." His smile faded, and he slammed his door. "Let's not talk about this anymore. I don't want the boys to know." He sighed. "They like you, Dani. It's hard to find a nanny they don't send screaming into the night."

"Fine." She closed her door. "Whatever happens is on you." She marched to the house, determined to do everything in her power to keep trouble away from the Rocking W. First, she needed to speak to her mother before she heard the news from Delly. She found her wiping the downstairs bathroom counter. "Got a minute?"

"Sure do." Her mother set the rag on the sink. "What's up?" She listened while Dani told her about the text messages. When she'd finished, her mother held out her hand. "Let me see them."

Dani dropped her phone into her mother's palm. "I went to the sheriff this morning. He's going to send someone to work undercover on the ranch."

"Good. That was the right decision you made."

She kept the news that it was Dylan's idea to herself.

"What's the plan?"

Dani shrugged. "I don't have one. We don't really know anything. Maybe these are idle threats."

"Nothing is ever that simple." Her mother picked up the cleaning rag. "Keep the boys close and stay on the ranch unless surrounded by cowboys packing guns."

Despite the severity of the situation, Dani laughed. "Not even a cowboy can stop a bullet."

"Maybe not, but you'll have something nice to look at before the bullet hits." Her mother grinned, then sobered. "In all seriousness, Danica, we'll be all right. We always are. Stay vigilant."

"Thanks, Mom. I'm going to see what the boys are up to." She headed upstairs and peeked in their room.

Their backpacks sat in the middle of their beds, but the boys were nowhere in sight. She closed their door and headed downstairs. Hopefully they were still having their after-school snack. When she didn't find them in the kitchen, her heart flew to her throat.

Shouts drifted through the kitchen screen door. Her heart rate returned to normal as she peered out to see the boys cheering on one of the cowboys perched in the saddle of a bucking horse. She'd never understood the excitement of the bone-jarring activity.

"Go on." Mrs. White stepped from the pantry. "I'm sure the boys would love to explain to you the fine points of bronc busting."

"Not interested." She grinned. "Since they are my responsibility, I'll pretend to be."

"Good girl. Heard we're getting a new cowboy by suppertime."

Dani glanced at the clock. "That isn't very long from now, but yes, I heard the same." If Dylan wanted the cook to know about the undercover cowboy, he could tell her. She pushed open the door and stepped onto the back deck.

"Howdy."

Dani gasped and jumped back, letting the screen door slam shut behind her. "You scared me, Willy. Why are you skulking around?"

He laughed. "Getting the empty bunk ready for the new guy. Boss told me the ladies would have clean bedding."

She gave a mock bow. "Please enter and see." Smiling, she straightened and headed for the corral.

"You should watch this, Dani." Eric glanced over his shoulder. "Dad is the best at staying in the saddle.

He even won a belt buckle once."

"Wow. A belt buckle." Which meant nothing to her, but she got the impression she should be impressed.

"Yeah. That means he's good."

She hadn't noticed it was Dylan on the back of the horse when she'd glanced out the window, but now that his cowboy hat lay in the dirt, she could see his handsome face set in determination. One gloved hand held the thingy on the saddle, and the other waved in the air. "How long will he stay on?"

"Until the horse stops bucking," Derrick said. "You don't know anything about ranching, do you?"

"Not really." She folded her arms on the top rail of the paddock. "Guess you two have all summer to teach me."

Eric snorted. "It'll take more than one summer."

Dani widened her eyes and stifled a giggle. The two boys really were too much.

The horse's bucking slowed, then stopped, and Dylan rode him at a slow trot around the paddock before sliding from the saddle and handing the reins to a waiting cowboy. He snatched his hat from the dirt, slapped it against his thigh, then smiled as he approached Dani and the boys.

"Nothing better for relieving stress than to have it pounded out of you." He set his hat in place.

"I'll do something else, thank you." Dani chuckled.

The bell signaling supper rang.

~

"Let's get cleaned up, boys." Dylan put a hand on the shoulder of each of his sons. "There should be a new ranch hand at the table for you to pester."

Rather than go in the house, he led the boys to a trough recently filled with water. Mrs. White didn't take kindly to dust in her kitchen. He hung his hat on a nearby tree, then splashed water over his face and neck. The boys took turns doing the same. Dylan glanced up to see Dani watching with an arched brow. "What?"

"I thought that only happened in the movies."

"Washing up this way? It's great when you don't have time for a shower and it's mealtime." Who wanted to stall when it was time to eat? It wasn't as if they were washing in dirty water.

Marilyn stepped onto the deck. "There you are. Make it snappy. You're making the new cowboy have to wait." Eyes wide, cheeks flushed, she dashed back into the house.

"Uh-oh." Dani grimaced. "The new guy must be handsome and close to her age. My mom has a soft spot for cowboys, and the look on her face says she's on the hunt. Plus, she's wearing lipstick."

"Should I tell the man to run?"

"I would."

Dylan laughed at the confused look on his sons' faces. "Just a joke, boys." He was eager to meet the man the sheriff thought could help keep the ranch safe.

"Meet Buster Jones." Marilyn's starry eyes gazed on the middle-aged man with salt-and-pepper hair cut short in a military style.

"Glad to have you here." Dylan thrust out his hand. "We'll talk after supper if that's all right with you."

"Absolutely." He returned Dylan's shake, nodded at Dani, then ruffled both boys' hair, seeming oblivious to the two older women's stares. Dylan sure hoped there wouldn't be trouble between the two women. He had enough to worry about without adding a kitchen rivalry.

Supper consisted of goulash and corn bread. Once he'd eaten and the women started clearing the table, Dylan asked Buster to follow him to his office. He closed the door behind them. "Have a seat, please." He folded his hands on the desktop. "I don't recognize you as one of the deputies."

"That's because I'm not. While most of Misty Hollow knows me, no newcomer will. I'm retired PD and sometimes hire myself out where I'm needed. Anyone who goes looking for a Deputy Jones won't find me." He grinned.

"Ever worked with horses before?"

"Not as a job, but my family had a couple when I was a kid. I know enough to fake it." He sobered and crossed his arms. "Don't worry, Mr. Wyatt. I'm good at what I do."

"Call me Dylan or Wyatt. Adding the mister is a dead giveaway." Having a retired PD working for him might be a good thing indeed. His reasoning made sense. "Have you told anyone?"

"Everyone I could. I thought it smart to let people think I got bored with retirement and hired on as temporary help for the summer. That way, if someone does go asking questions, well…it ain't far from the truth, now is it?"

Dylan chuckled. "I don't guess so. Always keep the lies at a minimum. My boys said they learned that truth from a friend at school." He stood. "Come on. I'll show you around. As far as the other men know, you're here helping out temporarily, just as you said. They won't question it."

"For a short while after retiring, I worked for a security firm. Mind if I make some safety suggestions while we're out walking around?"

"Not at all." He'd do whatever it took to keep his children and hired hands safe for as long as the funds held out. Hopefully, his grand plans of camps and tours would give him a nice padding in his bank account by the summer's end, and the person behind the text messages to Dani turned out to be more bark than bite.

"The sheriff said someone watched from the woods?" Buster stopped and stared in that direction. "I'm thinking you might want some motion lights out there that warn you inside the house that someone is prowling around."

Dylan heard the cha-ching of dropping money. "We've got a dog."

"Need more than one. Get a donkey, too. Nothing nosier when strangers are around." He chuckled. "Of course, it'll be hee-hawing a lot with folks traipsing around your property seeking a taste of ranch life."

"I think I'll hold off on the donkey for a while."

"I wouldn't. Still a great warning system. It'll figure out friend from foe soon enough. I have a friend who will give you one free of charge. Clarence is on the old side but still spunky."

"All right." The boys were always hounding him for more animals on the ranch. They'd have the old girl spoiled within a day. "What else?"

"Camera at the front entrance under your sign. That way you have a record of every person and vehicle that comes on your property." He faced Dylan. "Ain't none of this going to come cheap, Boss, but I know a guy who will do a payment plan if that makes it easier."

Could Buster read minds? "That would be a big help."

"This is a new ranch. It takes time to make money at it. You'll get there." He clapped Dylan on the shoulder and headed for the barn.

His words did little to dispel the dark cloud hanging over Dylan's head. He'd wanted to install a security system since purchasing the ranch but thought he had some time.

"You got a safe room?"

His shoulders slumped. "No. Is one really necessary?"

"I reckon not, but they're always nice if someone sets the house on fire or armed men storm the place."

Dylan frowned and stared at the man's profile. He wasn't a retired police officer. The man was paranoid. Being ex-military PD himself, Dylan knew when to be worried, but he came nowhere near this man. Was his desire for success causing him to wear blinders since finding out about Dani's trouble?

Chapter Seven

Dani woke the next morning to feet thundering past her room. She groaned and glanced at her watch. First day of summer camp, and she'd been assigned the wonderful task of making sure Eric and Derrick behaved while giving their classmates a tour. There wouldn't be enough coffee on the ranch for that task.

She tossed aside the sheet she'd covered up with and padded to the shower. The boys would be busy with breakfast, hopefully, long enough. If not, her mother would keep an eye on them until Dani reached the kitchen. The hot water washed away the sleep, making her more coherent before joining the others.

Her mother glanced over from the stove. "Breakfast isn't for another fifteen minutes, but the boys couldn't wait. Would you like your pancakes now?"

"Just coffee and toast for me, Mom. Thanks." Another glance at the watch showed an hour until the front gate opened for business. "It's going to be a rush feeding the men and cleaning up before the guests arrive."

"No guests in the big house today. Dylan is working on a new meal schedule as we speak." She elbowed Mrs. White. "Buster is coming." Her mother then smoothed her hair and the pink apron she wore.

Good grief. Dani shook her head and prepared her own toast and coffee before sitting at the table across from the boys. "Mornin'."

The boys scowled for a few seconds before Eric spoke. "We thought you were going to sleep all day."

"It's a little past seven. Not late at all." She curled her hands around her coffee mug. "I'm as excited as you to start the day."

"Think of all the new people!" Derrick jabbed his syrup-dripping fork toward the sky.

That's what bothered Dani the most. Not the children who would be visiting, but the adults. Although there wouldn't be any overnight camping for a few weeks, there would be adults scoping out the place. She'd have to be vigilant, watching not only two rowdy boys, but the possible target on her back.

A meager breakfast over and twin boys trembling with excitement, Dani followed them onto the front porch where they stared at the road leading to the house. Monster joined them. Nursing her second cup of coffee, Dani lowered into a chair and propped her feet on a padded ottoman. The day would be busy enough without wanting it to come earlier.

"Good morning." Dylan came around the corner of the house. "I thought I might find y'all out here."

"The boys can't wait." She smiled. "Me? Barely awake."

"You'll wake up soon enough when twenty-five ten-year-olds show up." He propped a booted foot on the top step. "Let's go over some rules, boys."

"Why do you have to go and ruin a good day?"

Derrick crossed his arms.

Dylan arched a brow. "It's rules or your room. Take your pick."

"Rules." Eric kicked his twin.

"Number one." Dylan held up a finger. "You stay with Dani at all times." He shook his head when the protests started. "We're all working in teams, son. The three of you are a team. Two. No going into the cowboys' bunkhouse. If your friends want to see it, they can peek in the window. Three. It's eat what the ladies cook or go hungry. Four. No venturing into the woods without me or Buster. Got it?"

"That all?" Derrick glowered.

"That and the rules you already live with day by day." He ruffled his son's hair. "I mean it, boys. We are going to have strangers here, and I don't want any trouble." His gaze met Dani's.

She nodded, recognizing the silent warning to be careful. "We'll be following your schedule with the guests and nothing else."

"Have fun." He turned and left the way he'd come.

When a school bus turned up the road, the boys dashed off the porch. Dani sighed and set her cup on the railing. She didn't mind two kids, but a whole classroom full was out of her comfort zone. Thankfully, two women and a man exited the bus before the kids.

The man strolled her way. "Hello. I'm the school principal, Mr. White."

"White? Is your mother the cook here?" Dani tilted her head.

"That's her. I'm going to pop in and say hi while you introduce yourself to the students." He jogged up the stairs and into the house.

"I'm a teacher, Susan Snodgrass, and this is a volunteer, Amy Warner. We're here to help."

"God bless you. I'm Dani Cooper, the nanny of these two. They're actually the ones in charge." She asked all the students to follow the twins' lead. "No wandering off. What a way to spend the first day of summer."

Susan shrugged. "We would have done it one day this past week, but Mr. Wyatt wasn't ready for us. The parents don't mind another day of freedom. Guaranteed, you'll see a lot of this bunch and others this summer."

Hopefully, the ranch had enough hands to manage. "Let's go to the barn. Boys?"

Heads up, chests puffed out, the twins led the group to the barn. Before they reached their destination, several vehicles pulled in front of the house, and Buster and a couple of the other cowboys greeted the arriving guests.

~

He scanned the area until his gaze landed on Dani Cooper entering the barn. The middle-aged cowboy standing on the steps droned on about all the ranch had to offer and how glad everyone was to see them, blah, blah, blah.

What he wanted to do was corner the woman and tell her to find a way to get his money. He needed funds in order to start his own empire. There was room for him now that the Robertos were gone.

The ranch owner took the other man's place and welcomed them all to the Rocking W and let them know overnight camping tours would start in two weeks. Anyone interested could sign up via the website address pinned to the porch railing. Well, he'd be the first to put down his name. The more time on the ranch, the better his chances of getting to Dani.

He wouldn't be as nice as the Robertos. Pay up or die. Those were the only options. Her death would show others he meant business.

~

After doing the ranch-owner task of greeting the guests, Dylan headed for the barn to check on the group of kids. With Dani, Mr. White, and the two women, he most likely wasn't needed, but he still wanted to make an appearance.

A wide-eyed Dani glanced over when he entered, then she made a beeline to his side. "Eric is offering horseback rides. I can't help with that."

"I'll ask a couple of the guys, don't worry. Since we haven't made time to complete your lessons yet—" something he needed to remedy, "there's no way I'll ask that of you. You need a lot more experience first."

"Thank you." She heaved a sigh. "It's bad enough they all want to feed the horses. Which ones are safe?"

"Did the boys show them how to keep their fingers out of the way?"

She nodded.

"Then, they're all safe. Even Lightning." The horse pushed his head against Dylan's shoulder. "He might be fearsome to ride, but otherwise, he's like a big puppy."

She gave the horse a timid pat on the muzzle, then rushed back to the group of children who had started throwing hay at each other. She clapped her hands three times, settling them down.

Impressive. Confident she had everything under control, Dylan went in search of a couple of men to give horseback rides.

Buster fell into step next to him. "Why do you think single men over the age of thirty-five would be interested in spending time on a ranch riding horses and camping? Kids I can understand."

"Something on your mind?" Dylan kept moving.

"Just what I said. I mean…these are mountain folk. Country people for the most part. This lifestyle isn't foreign to them."

"I know for a fact we have some guests from Little Rock and Fort Smith. Maybe this is as simple as them marking off a bucket-list item. Not everyone rode horses as a kid or had the chance to go camping." Spotting Ryder tossing hay to the horses in the paddock, he switched directions.

"Okay, but I'm keeping a close eye on the three single men here." Buster veered off.

A few minutes later, Ryder and River had been assigned the task of giving horseback rides around one of the paddocks. Dylan then headed for the kitchen. He still hadn't had time to give Mrs. White the meal schedule for the days they had guests.

In the kitchen, he pulled a folded sheet of paper from the pocket of his jeans. "Sorry. I know we didn't serve breakfast, but I would like to do lunch for this crowd. They'll be gone by supper. I'll give you two days' notice from now on, I promise." He handed Mrs. White the schedule.

"Good thing we've already made some patties for burgers and pulled out hotdogs. Marilyn put a potato salad in the fridge. Deviled eggs and pasta salad coming right up—" She glanced at the clock. "Ready for lunch in an hour."

"You are a blessing." The woman had come with the ranch, sort of, showing up on his doorstep after a few days, saying she'd worked for the previous owner. Dylan couldn't be happier. If he slacked on something, she'd pick it right up and keep moving.

By the time he returned outside, two lines had formed for children to ride the horses, and another for the smaller number of adults. Maybe Buster was right. It did seem strange to see grown men standing in line like the kids. He shrugged. It wasn't his place to wonder why, only to make sure they got what they paid for. He smiled and nodded, then leaned on the corral railing to watch.

One of the male guests stepped into the corral, then hesitated. "I've never ridden before."

"Nothing to it," Willy said. "Put that foot there and swing that leg over. Want me to lead you?"

"No, I can manage inside the corral." The man climbed clumsily into the saddle and almost slid off the other side.

Dylan ducked his head to stifle a grin. He turned his attention back to the line. One of the three men was missing. He glanced toward the bathroom door he'd installed on the outside of the guest bunkhouse, giving access from the inside or out. When no one came out after a few minutes, he pushed away from the corral and headed in that direction.

The man was nowhere near the bunkhouse or the barn. Dylan stared toward the main house. Not seeing anyone stirring there either, he did a search around the perimeter. When he circled back to the house, he spotted the missing man peering through one of the downstairs windows.

"Can I help you?" He stopped a couple of feet from the man.

"I'm looking for the bathroom."

"Were you not here when the others were told it's the door on the east side of the bunkhouse?" Dylan set his jaw.

The man gave a sheepish grin and a shrug. "Guess I wasn't paying attention. My apologies. The aromas coming from the house sure do smell good."

"We'll be eating under that canopy over there at noon." Dylan tipped his hat and watched the man rush away. He studied the area until his gaze landed on Buster who stepped from the shadows of the bunkhouse.

Buster nodded in Dylan's direction, then pointed at his own eyes with two fingers, then at the retreating man. He'd been watching the man all along.

Chapter Eight

Dani settled the boys at the table designated for the school kids, then glanced at the other table under the large white canopy. Mrs. White and Dani's mother carried platters piled with burgers, hotdogs, and homemade fries to the table.

Children's laughter filled the air along with the chatter of adults reaching for plates and utensils. Dani peered at Dylan. Her smile faded at the hard glint in his eye as he stared at one of the men sitting toward the end of the table.

The man seemed oblivious to Dylan's attention as he loaded his burger with onions and tomato. Her gaze slid to Buster Brown. He, too, watched the man. Why this man? What had he done? Her blood chilled, and her gaze flicked back to Dylan.

Dylan's smile didn't quite reach his eyes as he headed her way. "Everything is fine."

"Is it? Because you and Buster are enough to scare me into next year." She squeezed ketchup onto the boys' plates.

"We're simply watching someone who was where he shouldn't have been. Just lost, I'm sure."

"Hmm." She narrowed her eyes. "You wouldn't be

sugarcoating something to spare my feelings, would you?"

He put a hand to his muscled chest. "Me?"

"Yes, you." She smiled despite the flickers of unease coursing through her. She glanced toward the man again. He wore his hat pulled low as if he didn't want anyone to get a good look at his face, but several of the ranch hands wore their hats the same way. Maybe the man wanted to copy them. "Okay, I believe you, but please don't withhold information from me."

He put a hand on her arm, sending bolts of electricity through her. "I won't."

She ducked her head, embarrassed at the rush of attraction she felt. "The boys and I will help clean all of this up once the guests leave at four." Next week would be a weeklong day camp for the students, and supper would be included. Thankfully, today was a shorter day to break everyone into the busier pace. From the weary lines on faces, she figured they all needed time to get used to the new way of things. Even the boys were slowing down.

After lunch, Willy led the children on a short hike into the woods. Those who didn't mind getting wet splashed in the creek. Dani sat cross-legged on a patch of grass and leaned back on her hands. She closed her eyes and lifted her face to a ray of sunshine dappling through the branches overhead.

The snap of a twig to her right made her eyes pop open. She straightened and studied the shadows. Nothing moved for several seconds, then the rustle of leaves made her breath hitch. She pushed slowly to her feet and moved closer to the group. Even a few feet could mean the difference between safety and danger.

As she reached the place next to the wiry Willy, Dani glanced over her shoulder.

"Something wrong?" He turned and looked in the same direction she did.

"I thought I heard something, but I didn't see anything."

"Could be nothing more than a squirrel, but I'll check it out. You stay here with the young'uns." He strode toward the tree line, his hand hovering over the gun on his hip.

She kept her gaze glued to his back until he stepped out of sight. Even then, she kept alternating her attention between the playing children and the cowboy.

"You seem nervous." The school principal, Mr. White, joined her.

"I'm not much of a…woodsy girl." She forced a smile. "I jump at every little noise."

He chuckled. "It won't take long for that to go away working out here."

"I hope not." She turned as Dylan approached on Lightning.

He glanced around, frowning as Willy stepped from the trees. With a nod at Dani and the principal, he slid from the saddle and headed in the cowboy's direction. The two conversed for a moment, then Dylan asked Dani to join him away from the others.

Her heart skipped a beat at the worry in his eyes. "Someone was out there, weren't they?"

"It looks that way. The tracks were too fresh to have been from the other day."

"Is anyone missing from the tour group?"

He shook his head. "The man we were watching never left the group again. It couldn't have been him."

"Should we head back?"

"I doubt anything will happen with so many people around. As long as you don't head anywhere alone, you should be safe." He tipped his hat back, revealing more of his face. "I'm serious about that, Dani. You don't go anywhere alone."

"I won't." Her gaze locked with his. She wanted to dive into those dark blue eyes and stay there hidden, where trouble couldn't touch her. Her eyes burned.

"Don't cry." He wrapped his strong arms around her. "I won't let anything happen to you."

She sniffed, pressing her forehead against his chest. "I know." At least, he'd do his best. No one could guarantee her safety. Not if the mob had resurfaced and wanted their pound of flesh from her.

What if someone else got hurt in the process of keeping her safe? She couldn't allow that. Dani stepped back and turned away. Anyone watching her would be hard-pressed to believe Dylan and his boys to be anything more to her than a job. But…they were becoming more with every hour of every day.

Was she a good enough actor to keep her feelings from showing?

~

He'd never get close to her. The ranch owner was on to something. Dani would constantly be surrounded by people. He melted further into the shadows, keeping his eye on the older cowboy and his boss. Even if he'd picked the older man off, that would have alerted those by the creek. No, for now he'd have to bide his time and continue signing up for whatever camping trips the ranch had scheduled. Eventually, his moment to confront Dani would come.

First, give her the warning about the money. If that didn't work, then he'd start making those around her pay, starting with her mother and sister. The sister wouldn't be difficult to get close to. Not at the diner. All he had to do was make sure her deputy husband wasn't nearby.

He laughed. He wouldn't mind ridding the world of one more lawmaker if the deputy did get in the way.

~

Dylan stayed with the children's group until they left at four, then helped Dani and the boys clean up the garbage left behind from the noon meal. The day had gone well, for the most part. All the guests seemed to have fun, and most of the adults signed up for the upcoming camping trip.

If not for the dark shadow of someone following Dani, the future looked bright indeed.

The worry line between her eyes urged him to smooth it away. The desire to see her smile tugged at him. "Want to sit on the deck with me after supper for a few moments of peace?"

Her eyes widened. "That would be nice. How do you propose getting away from the twins?"

"They'll crash in front of the television. Look at them." He motioned his head to where his sons moved in slow motion. "Playing tour guide wore them out."

"Poor things. I have to admit to being tired myself." She tied a large garbage closed just as the supper bell rang. "At least we don't have to clean up after this meal."

"I may have to hire an extra person just to help with cleanup." Even his shoulders ached from the work of the day.

Their steps fell in tune with each other as they ushered the boys into the main house. The twins headed for one bathroom to wash, while Dylan and Dani headed to another. No rushed wash in the trough today. He needed soap and hot water.

Supper was a simple casserole. Conversation stayed at the minimum. Once everyone had eaten and carried their dishes into the kitchen, the ranch hands excused themselves and headed for the evening chores before bunking down.

Dylan settled the twins in the living room, then poured two cups of coffee before joining Dani on the back deck. He chuckled to see coffee already poured and waiting for him. "Great minds think alike."

"The way I'm feeling, I might need two cups." She smiled and blew into the mug she held. "I could make sitting out here a nightly routine. It's beautiful."

He agreed. Being so high on the mountain, the sun seemed to set early, kissing the tops of trees and stretching the shadows toward the house. Maybe it could become a routine between him and Dani.

What was he thinking? As a single father with a new ranch to run and needing a lot of funds in order to care for the ranch and his family, there was no time for a relationship. Not for a good long while, anyway. Could he be content to be nothing more than friends with his sons' nanny? Especially one whom trouble followed?

Still, he hadn't been attracted to another woman since his wife's death. He'd dated a time or two, but none of them made him want to spend his evenings on the back deck drinking coffee, just the two of them with plans to continue doing so.

He turned his head and caught her watching him with eyes the color of a summer meadow. Green with flecks of gold like wildflowers. Full lips and corn-silk hair. He found himself wanting very much to kiss her. To forget all the reasons why doing so was a bad idea.

"Do you think we're being watched right now?" She asked softly.

He jerked upright. "What?"

She repeated herself.

"Possibly." He put two fingers to his lips and whistled. Within seconds, Monster climbed from under the deck. "Search, boy."

The dog yawned, then took off for the woods. Dylan really needed to send the dog out more or consider buying a couple more. The ranch was too large for one dog to monitor, especially an aging one like Monster.

"No one can get to you while you're on the ranch." He reached over and placed his hand on her arm. "Too many people. Too many animals." He told her about Buster's suggestion regarding a donkey and more dogs.

"I love donkeys." She smiled and reached for coffee cup number two. "This will probably keep me up tonight, but Mrs. White makes good coffee."

Relieved to be pulled back to being sensible and not romantic, he nodded and turned his attention to the tree line. Monster couldn't talk, but he'd bark if anyone watched them. The deck sat back too far for anyone armed with anything other than a sniper rifle to reach. He didn't think whoever was after Dani wanted her dead. If they did, she'd already be dead. No, they wanted something she didn't have. Something he couldn't help her with in his current financial situation.

He doubted Marilyn could either. At this point, all they could do was wait and hope the sheriff's department brought down the bad guys when they showed their ugly faces. That, and pray Dani and his boys didn't get caught in the crosshairs.

Chapter Nine

Two weeks, Dani. You have two weeks to get my money. One hundred thousand dollars. Get it and keep it within reach. You never know when I'll come. Just know that I am always close.

Dani dropped to her bed, legs weak. How close? As in on the ranch? No, Dylan trusted all the ranch hands.

She jumped to her feet and rushed to the window. An hour before breakfast, the twins were still asleep, and the cowboys just starting to stir. Dylan trusted his men. Her stalker couldn't be one of them. Then who?

She wracked her brain running through all the faces she'd met in New York while spending time with the Robertos. Stephanie Roberto, the daughter, had had a couple of suitors, one a fiancé, the other a side dalliance. The fiancé would have the most to lose with her gone.

Chewing the inside of her bottom lip, Dani headed downstairs to find Dylan. He glanced up from his desk when she knocked on his open office door. "Do you have a minute?"

"Absolutely." He smiled.

"I received another text." She held out her phone

as his smile faded.

He read the message, his brow furrowing. "We need to let Buster and the sheriff know."

"This person has been on the ranch, Dylan. Might still be here."

He shook his head. "I think he comes as a guest. We'll have to keep an eye on any regulars. When we're full, I'll do my best to stay close to you and the boys."

"I don't want you and your children in danger." Her throat clogged. "It's time for me to go, Dylan. I can't stay here." The thought was like a knife to the gut.

"Go where?" A muscle ticked in his jaw.

"Somewhere far from here."

"You came to Misty Hollow months ago thinking trouble couldn't find you and it did. There is nowhere you can run."

"Witness Protection." She crossed her arms.

He exhaled sharply. "You say you don't want anyone to be harmed. We're already in the crosshairs. If you leave, you'll just introduce trouble to a new group of people. We'll take care of this, I promise." He scooted his chair back and stood, then moved a few inches from her. "No more talk about leaving."

Her phone dinged again.

Don't think I won't make someone pay if I don't get my money.

Anyone. Your mother, the boys, the cowboy.

"How about now?" She held her phone where he could see.

He paled, and his eyes flashed. "Even now. You aren't going anywhere. This ranch is the safest place for you. I believe that."

She searched his face for a hint of the resolve that

kept him confident. Just a breath of it might be enough to get her through this. She gave a slow nod, knowing that if she caught a glimpse of danger too close at hand, too close to the twins, she'd run as far and as fast as she could.

"Come on." He took her hand. "We're going to have a group of hyper ten-year-olds here soon for riding and roping lessons. You'll be so busy every day this week you won't have time to worry about someone sending you texts."

The crease in his brow didn't quite cement the lie. Still, he tried, and for that she was grateful. "I'll wake the twins up and meet you in the kitchen."

Dani stood in the doorway of the boys' room and watched them sleep for several moments before moving to the side of the bed and gently shaking them awake. "Come on, sleepyheads. We've got a big day ahead of us." She stepped to the window and shoved aside the curtains.

She frowned. A dirty handprint, too large to belong to one of the twins marred the windowsill. She leaned out and stared at the ground under the window. Two floors below, but she could make out a set of footprints. An adult male could possibly climb the trellis. Her heart dropped to her knees. Had someone watched the boys sleep during the night? She needed to speak to Dylan. Again. Now. "Get up, boys. I'll see you at breakfast in ten minutes." She rushed from the room and thundered down the stairs. "Dylan!"

He exited his office. "What's wrong?"

"Someone was outside the boys' room last night. They left a handprint on the sill and footprints outside." She made a dash for the front door.

"Whoa." His hand shot out to stop her. "I'll go first. Wait right here." He ducked back into his office, remerging with his handgun and his cell phone to his ear. "Buster, meet me on the west side of the main house. Now, please." Motioning for Dani to stay behind him, Dylan opened the front door and stepped onto the porch. After a few tense seconds, he jumped off the steps and headed around the house, Dani so close behind she could reach out and touch him.

When he stopped suddenly, she rammed into him, then stepped back and rubbed her nose. "Sorry."

He made a noise in his throat, then squatted to study the set of footprints. "Size eleven, gym shoes. Looks like a common enough tread." Planting his hands on his thighs, he straightened and glanced up at the window where his sons both peered down.

"What 'cha doin', Dad?" Eric leaned so far out Dani gasped.

"Go back inside and get ready for breakfast like I told you!"

Eyes wide, both boys pulled back.

"Wow." The corner of Dylan's mouth quirked. "When you bark, they respond."

"I've never yelled at them like that before, but he scared me. I'm sorry."

"Don't be. Hold this." He handed her his gun, then shimmied up the trellis as if it were the easiest thing in the world.

Footsteps sounded behind her.

She whirled and aimed the gun.

"Watch out." Buster swiped it from her. "You don't want to go and shoot the wrong person."

~

Dylan compared the handprint on the windowsill to his own, then joined the others on the ground. "The man appears to be my size, down to his shoe size." He explained that someone had been looking in the window sometime before morning.

"I suggest you put locks on all the windows." Buster glanced upward. "Thought anymore about my security suggestions?"

"Yes. Let's get the ball rolling. I've a bunch of ten-year-olds arriving today, but I can get one of the other men to help Dani while I help you." He took his gun and shoved it into the waistband of his pants. Hand on the small of Dani's back, he guided her back inside. "Not a word to the others."

"Okay." She nodded and headed to help her mother and Mrs. White set the table.

The boys clambered down the stairs soon after, sniffing the air like dogs. "Bacon!"

Dylan chuckled. They'd already forgotten their question as to what he'd been doing outside their window. Good. They'd ask too many questions otherwise—ones he wasn't prepared to answer. He turned to Buster. "Let's take breakfast to my office and make those calls."

"Will do. I can get someone out here fast. Cameras, alarms, you got it."

"Don't forget the donkey and the dogs." He was going to be as prepared as possible. "The camp kids will love the donkey. We'll say that's why we've brought one to the ranch."

"The dogs won't be pets, Dylan. Best keep the young'uns away from them."

Dylan nodded, not liking the idea of hostile

animals around the children. "I can't have that kind of liability."

"We'll ask for ones that get along with kids. I'm only being cautious." Buster filled his plate, reaching around the other cowboys, then headed for the office.

Dylan made his apologies, then did the same. He hated leaving Dani to handle the kids without him, but Willy would be a good stand-in.

In the office, he sat back and ate while Buster made the necessary calls. When he'd finished, he grinned. "This place will be hopping within the hour."

"Some folks must've owed you a few favors."

"One or two." His smile faded. "I don't like that this scoundrel got so close to the boys, Dylan. I'm going to have to let the sheriff know. Might not hurt to bring another deputy or two out here undercover."

"Whoever this perp is, he's been on the ranch enough to know the faces of my hands. If we bring on two more…" Dylan sighed. "It might tip him off."

"It might. But we would also have more guns ready. Your call." He dug into the breakfast he'd set aside. "As for me, well, I'd bring in the extra men."

"The dogs will be good to patrol at night. What do you think about a couple of deputies here as part of the camping trips and adult day camps?"

"That would work. I'll see what the sheriff thinks and get back to you."

The gleeful shouting of ten-year-olds drifted through the open window, soon joined by greetings from his boys. "I'm going to say howdy until the security people arrive. Hunt me down when they do."

"Will do." Buster grabbed both his and Dylan's plates and headed for the kitchen.

A little over an hour later, a white panel van, followed by an SUV and a horse trailer, pulled in front of the barn. Dylan excused himself from the horseback-riding lessons with promises to introduce the kids to a new friend, then went to greet his new security team.

"This is Clarence." A man in coveralls backed a donkey from the trailer. "Two-years-old and as cantankerous as a bear woken up from hibernation. A sugar cube calms him right down."

"How is he with strangers? I was expecting an older mule."

"That one wasn't available after all. This one is horrible. He'll bray loud enough to wake the dead. Give him a day or two, and he'll know who belongs here and who doesn't. I have Heidi and Sadie in the SUV. Two mixed-breed females. You couldn't ask for better watchdogs." He nodded to where Monster sniffed around the vehicle. "They'll boss him around for sure, poor thing."

"As long as they realize he was here first." Dylan grinned, already feeling a thousand times safer. He turned as men carrying rolls of wiring moved toward the house.

"If you ever feel you don't need these girls anymore, we'll buy them back from you. Seems like there's always a need for good dogs on farms and ranches." The man opened the back door of the SUV, and two brindle dogs jumped out. "Hey, girls, meet your new master."

Dylan held out his hand. Once the sniffing was over, he patted both heads and called Monster over. "How are they with kids?"

"They'll stay away from them for the most part,

but they won't attack. Just don't let anyone go hanging on them. They don't like that. These girls aren't cuddlers." He handed the donkey's reins to him. "This boy loves kids."

"Thanks." Dylan gripped the lead rope and led the donkey to the group of children by the corral.

~

He watched from the woods. Things were becoming a whole lot harder. Getting close wouldn't be easy with two more dogs and a security system. Still, the upcoming camping trip should provide the opportunity he needed.

Stupid woman didn't appear to be trying to get her hands on any money. Dani had done it before with the help of her mother, then she didn't have to pay a dime because of the fall of the Roberto family. If she could do it once, she could do it again.

Shoot. The rancher would pay the money himself in order to keep his boys safe. Why else threaten the kids? He didn't have a beef with them, only the woman and all he wanted from her was the money. She hadn't been the only one in hock because of gambling debts. If he didn't pay up soon, he'd be at the bottom of Misty Mountain Lake, with no one the wiser.

Being alone in the world held no merits.

He cursed and marched away from the ranch and down the logging road where he'd parked the rental truck. An older model as dilapidated as many he saw around Misty Hollow. A vehicle that helped him blend in.

In the driver's seat, he turned the key in the ignition and tried to devise a plan to meet his goal of staying alive past the end of the month.

If he died, so would Dani Cooper. He didn't plan on going down alone.

Chapter Ten

Dani smiled as Clarence ate a carrot from her hand. The boys had fist-bumped each other when their father had told them about the new addition to the ranch. The dogs had held a mild interest, but unless one of the females had puppies, they didn't seem to care as much about them as about the donkey. "You're supposed to warn us when the bad guys come, huh?" She patted his nose. "You don't seem so tough."

"Let a coyote wander into the pasture, and you'll see how tough he is." Buster hung a halter on the fence post. "Cattle ranchers keep donkeys all the time. They can be brutal and noisy."

She crossed her arms on the top rail and rested her chin on them, her gaze on the grazing donkey. "I hope all the measures you've put into place will be enough."

"Chin up, buttercup. You've been through this before, and you came out okay." He clapped her on the shoulder, before continuing on his way.

Dani wished she shared his optimism. If there weren't others in danger, maybe she'd have more faith. "I really hope you do your job, boy." She pushed away from the paddock and went to get the boys ready for the soon-to-arrive group of schoolkids. "Good job, boys."

She grabbed a pitchfork and helped feed the horses in the stalls.

"It's not fair that we have to shovel horse manure first thing in the morning." Derrick leaned on his shovel.

"You don't want your friends to step in the stuff, do you?" She arched a brow. "Besides, shoveling horse doo is on the list of summer chores your father gave you."

"Where's your list?" Eric glared.

"My job is to make sure you do yours." She grinned and hefted another pitchfork of hay over a stall door. "Chores are a blessing—they keep you from being lazy."

"Ha," they said in unison.

As the squeak of bus brakes sounded outside, they leaned their shovels against the wall, each grabbed a wheelbarrow full of manure, then raced as fast as they could out the door without toppling the wheelbarrow.

"Don't forget to wash up before greeting your friends." Dani took over and pushed each wheelbarrow out of sight around the barn. One of the cowboys would dump them later. She glanced around for any unfamiliar face as she'd started to do each day, then joined the boys at the water pump to wash her hands. "You two seem to really be enjoying having your classmates here each day." She lathered her hands with soap.

"Beats all-day chores or watching TV." Eric flung water from his hands, then dashed toward the rented bus where his friends had gathered.

"We like being boss." Derrick flashed a grin, then joined his brother.

Boss, huh? She chuckled. Yes, they did seem to

enjoy telling their friends what to do and how to do it.

Heidi and Sadie sped past her, barking. Clarence brayed.

Dani's heart leaped into her throat, and she whirled toward the ruckus.

An armadillo froze near the horse paddock, then curled into a ball. Dani rushed to intercept the poor thing before the dogs tore it apart.

"Hold up." Dylan sprinted past her. "The claws on that thing will tear you apart." He set a metal trap in front of it and called off the dogs before ushering the animal inside. He closed the trapdoor and faced her. "Wild animals don't take kindly to being saved. Especially, if they're frightened."

"What are you going to do with it?" She wasn't exactly sure how she would've helped the animal, but she hadn't intended on picking it up with her bare hands.

"Release it away from the ranch. They dig too many holes." He flashed a grin and marched past her, tossing over his shoulder that he'd let the kids all take a peek before sending it away.

Her heart rate slowly returned to normal as she scanned the tree line. The three dogs ambled around the paddock, nose to the ground. Clarence had returned to grazing. All seemed right on the ranch. So, why did the hairs on the back of her neck still stand at attention?
She needed to formulate an escape plan in case the worst happened. Willy was teaching the children how to start a fire from scratch. They'd be busy for a bit.

Chewing her thumbnail, she headed back to the barn and stared at Daisy. There hadn't been nearly enough riding lessons—something she planned on changing. She also wasn't comfortable putting the saddle on the horse.

Dani lowered to a three-legged stool to make a plan. She knew where the keys to the ranch vehicles were, but they weren't always accessible. Not with as many hands as the ranch had. Okay, she had two potential modes of transportation. She could flee via the road if she had a vehicle or across the land on a four-wheeler or horse. The next thing she would need would be a weapon.

The gun she'd purchased months ago was locked in the safe in the camper. She'd need to find a place where she'd have easy access to the weapon but keep it out of the twins' reach. Money was also an issue. Cash on hand would be necessary. A frustrated sigh came out. She and the boys would be required to attend the overnight camping trips. A rapid escape would be near impossible.

Dani slapped her hands against her thighs and stood. She'd figure it out—she always did. Feeling better with the semblance of a plan if things went south, Dani left the barn and joined the boys and their friends.

~

The children oohed and aahed over the armadillo before Dylan handed it over to Colt to dispose of somewhere away from the ranch. Dylan glanced up as Dani joined them. "Sorry, I barked at you. Guess I'm too used to telling the boys to stay back and don't touch."

She shrugged. "No big deal." A shadow crossed her features.

"I really am sorry." He hadn't meant anything by his words.

Her gaze flicked to his. "It's okay, really."

He narrowed his eyes. What was going through her pretty head? He didn't think he'd like whatever thoughts flittered there. "Walk with me."

"The boys—"

"For a minute." Once they were away from the others, he stopped and faced her. "What's on your mind?"

"Riding lessons." She lifted her chin.

"Riding lessons?"

"Yes."

"Okay." With everything else, her lessons had been allowed to slide. "We'll resume this weekend, or would you prefer the evenings after the kids have left?"

"Whenever you have time is fine with me. All we've done is get me in the saddle."

"You're right. I'm sorry. I should've made riding a priority." He frowned, studying her face and the way she refused to make eye contact. "Anything else?"

"No, that's it. Thanks." She gave a quick smile that didn't seem the slightest bit sincere.

He thought they'd been growing close. What happened? "Have you received another text?"

"No, thank goodness." She glanced over as Willy demonstrated how to douse the fire they'd just built. "I should get back to work." She turned to leave.

"Dani?" He reached out to stop her but let his hand drop. "Okay."

The air grew chillier as she moved away. Dread filled his heart. He knew deep inside she planned on leaving. Somehow, someday, he'd look up and she'd be gone.

"Boss, got a minute?" Deacon Simpson, one of his

hands, called to him from the barn.

After one final glance at Dani's back, Dylan headed for the barn. "What's up? The boys didn't do their chores?"

"No, they did. I was getting ready to spread the manure and found something I thought you might want to see." He jerked his head around the corner of the building.

What now? Dylan's steps dragged as he followed.

"The prints aren't fresh. More like a day or two old." Deacon drew Dylan's attention to the soil under the barn window.

The prints were the same as the ones under the window belonging to the boys' room. His blood heated. This perp seemed as interested in the boys as he was in Dani. Dylan's fingers curled, itching to wrap around the unknown man's neck.

"What do you want to do?"

He rolled his head on his shoulders. "Guess we need to start shifts at patrolling the ranch at night. We'll do our best to stay out of sight. There are enough of us that it shouldn't disturb our sleep too much."

Deacon nodded. "I'll have all of us draw straws for the order. Want us armed or not?"

"Armed. All the time." He spun and marched for the main house. Time to fill the women in on what had been happening. Everyone needed to be on guard. "Ladies." The screen banged shut behind him as he entered the house. "I'd like to speak to both of you. Please, have a seat." He motioned to the small kitchen dinette.

Mrs. White wiped her flour-covered hands on a towel. "Sounds serious."

"It is. Marilyn?"

"If this is about the trouble my daughter brought onto the ranch, I've already filled Lenora in." Marilyn hung her towel over her shoulder and sat.

"There's more than that. We've had someone skulking around at night. That's the reason for the additional dogs, security system, and the donkey." He still thought it funny to consider Clarence part of the security team. "Someone has been watching my boys."

Marilyn frowned. "Not Dani?"

"We've only found footprints under the boys' window and by the barn. I'm sure this person is also watching Dani, but he also wants my boys." A cold hand gripped his heart.

"To get at my girl. He knows she'll do anything to protect those boys." Marilyn squared her shoulders. "What do you need us to do?"

"Keep your eyes open and a gun in your apron pocket. I trust you to keep any firearms out of the hands of children, but we need to be prepared to defend this place. It's all hands at the ready."

The women nodded.

"Mrs. White, Marilyn, if you want to leave, no one will blame either of you."

"Not a chance. My girl needs me." Marilyn crossed her arms.

"This is my home, same as yours." Mrs. White's eyes flashed. "It's also about time you call me Lenora, don't you think? No, sir, we're all in this together."

"I couldn't ask for better friends and workers." He took one of each of their hands in his. "You ladies are the best. If you do see something, let me or Buster know. Do not approach the suspect yourself.

Understand?"

Marilyn grinned. "I'll be happy to call Buster for just about anything."

His mood lifted a bit, and Dylan released their hands. "Let's not say anything around the boys, and please keep an eye on Dani. I suspect she's planning to flee."

"You leave her to me." Her mother frowned. "Dani is headstrong, for sure, but I'll make her see reason. Guaranteed."

"Don't let her know I said anything." He didn't want her avoiding him more than she already was.

Satisfied that everyone on the ranch would be as alert as they could be, Dylan stepped back outside to the sound of children's laughter. He could almost believe evil would stay away, the kids' joy chasing it into the shadows.

But no, his time in the military, then as a widower, watching his wife die in his arms after falling from her horse and hitting her head—Dylan knew happiness could be fleeting and just out of reach. Still, he held onto hope that someday light and love would once again fill his heart.

Chapter Eleven

Dani's blood boiled as she listened to her mother make a list of "rules" during Sunday lunch at the diner. Today was one of Dani's few days off since the ranch had started day camps. Her mother had insisted that she, Dani, and Delly have lunch together on Sunday.

"Basically, you want to lock me in my room until the bad guy is caught." Dani crossed her arms and glared.

"Not exactly, but sort of, yes." Mom didn't seem rattled by her attitude. "Our Sunday lunches at Lucy's will have to stop, too. Delly can come to the ranch to spend time with us."

"Joey isn't keen on me being anywhere near Dani." Delly stirred cream into her coffee.

"He'd keep you away from your own sister?" Dani turned her glare on her twin.

"No, but he will try and keep me away from danger." Her gaze met Dani's. "I was almost killed three months ago, remember?"

"Only because you insisted on pretending to be me." Dani's eyes burned. "I didn't ask for this. I paid my debt to society months ago. Just because I've made bad choices in the past doesn't mean they have to follow me my whole life, do they? Aren't I entitled to a normal life?" Their faces swam in front of her tears. "I should just leave."

"Absolutely not. We're a family, and we're in this together." Her mother hitched her chin, eyes flashing. "We just need some…guidelines in order to keep you alive."

"Joey is afraid I'll be mistaken for Dani again." Delly took a sip of her coffee. "I suggested cutting my hair, but he was completely against that idea."

"Whoever is watching me will be able to tell the difference by now." Dani sighed. When would the nightmare of her gambling addiction be behind her?

"Worst case scenario, I still have the money we came up with to pay off Roberto." Mom folded her hands on the table. "I bet we can convince Dylan to pitch in to keep his boys safe."

"No. This isn't his problem." She absolutely refused to get him involved any more than he already was.

"It became his problem the moment he hired you."

Ouch. "Another reason for me to leave."

"You'd never survive on your own."

"Witness protection."

"That doesn't always work." Her mother put a hand over Dani's. "You used to trust me to know what was best. Why can't you now? This isn't an argument you're going to win, sweetie."

"I'm no longer a child, Mom."

"You can still trust me."

She straightened, removing her hand. "I won't run, but I do have escape plans in place, and I want my gun from the safe." She sniffed and wiped her eyes with a napkin. "I'll keep it away from the boys, but—"

"Dylan told me and Lenora to carry ours with us, so you should pack as well." She shrugged. "He's expecting a gunfight."

Delly spewed her coffee. "Sorry, but you can't be serious. He's just preparing for the worst-case scenario. It's not like we're fighting the mob again. The Robertos were shut down."

"There is always someone willing to take their place." Mom set some cash on the table. "Evil doesn't rest. Whoever is after that cash has put us all in jeopardy. If we're vigilant and do what the authorities say, we'll come out ahead. Just like before."

Dani prayed she was right because at this point she was starting to lose hope. The deadline loomed like a speeding train getting closer with each minute. "If the lecture is over, I'd like to return to the ranch. I have another riding lesson today." It would be the first time out of the paddock. Becoming adept at horseback riding could be the difference between life and death for her.

"Fine." Mom slid from the booth, gave Delly a hug, then followed Dani to the truck where she climbed into the passenger seat. "Nice of Dylan to give you the use of a vehicle. You do realize that escaping in his truck or on his horse would be stealing, right?"

Dani rolled her eyes. "Yes, Mom." But that wouldn't stop her if it meant keeping the others safe. She turned the key in the ignition and thrust the truck into park. A glance in her rearview mirror had her hit the brake instead of the gas. What now?

Joey exited his squad car and tapped on the driver's side window of the truck. "How are you two?"

"Peachy." Dani forced a smile. "Heard you didn't want my twin around me."

He pressed his lips together, then sighed. "It isn't personal, Danica. I'm only concerned for my wife's safety."

"So am I." She squared her shoulders. "Why don't you just lock my sister in your house until this is all over?" She started to roll up the window. "One less target for a madman."

"You're being unreasonable."

"Yep." She was tired of other people thinking she would make another bonehead decision that ended up killing someone. "It's a talent. Please move your car. I have an appointment."

He glanced past her to her mother. "Try talking some sense into her, would you, Marilyn?"

"I'm trying, but it isn't easy. The best thing for everyone is to keep Dani at the ranch and close to the house. Heard you might be coming by once in a while."

"Plan on it. The sheriff wants as many eyes on the ranch visitors as possible. I'm not opposed to some overtime if it involves horses." He grinned and slapped the hood of the truck. "See y'all. Use your head and stay safe." He marched to his car and backed from the lot.

Dani exhaled heavily and rolled her head on tense shoulders. "I'm getting tired of being treated like an idiot." She jammed her foot on the gas and peeled rubber from the parking lot.

"Speeding isn't going to help your cause, dear." Mom gripped the handle hanging near her head.

Dani slowed. "I'm not the same person I was three months ago, Mom. You forget that I proved my intelligence and bravery during that time, too. Now is no different. I'm not going to do anything stupid that will put anyone's life in danger. Just doing my job, that's it."

"You're right, and I'm sorry. We shouldn't be treating you like a wayward child."

"Thank you." She cut her mother a quick glance, then smiled. "Maybe we should set a trap like we did before."

"I've been thinking about that, but don't tell your sister." Mom grinned. "When we can, you and I will put our heads together and come up with a plan. We'll get this guy, Dani. Just like we brought down Roberto."

Hope leaped in her. "Yes, we will." They'd have to do it without involving Dylan or the boys. Maybe they could draw out the bad guy and lure him away from the ranch. She parked the truck in front of the house and headed for the barn while her mother went inside. It might be Sunday and their day off, but there were still meals to cook. As for the boys, Dylan took over on Sunday.

Eric and Derrick sat on bales of hay in the barn while Dylan saddled Daisy. "We're going to head for the woods today. Take a ride along the creek. Sound good?" He smiled.

She nodded, her throat dry. "Sure." She coughed and tried again. "Sounds fun."

"We're going, too." The boys jumped up and ran to her. "Dad said we'll take a picnic."

"I've already eaten."

"Then you can sit there and watch us eat." Dylan handed her the reins to her horse. "Lead her outside. We'll be right there."

Okay. Surprisingly enough, the horse followed as Dani headed outside. She led her to the stump, determined to get into the saddle on her own. "Now, you stay still. Don't make me fall." She glanced around to see whether anyone was watching, then climbed on the stump. Taking a deep breath, she put her left foot in the stirrup and swung her right leg over, settling her rump in the saddle. "I did it!"

Daisy tossed her head and danced away from the stump.

"Whoa!" Dani gripped the reins tighter.

~

Dylan's eyes widened at the sight of Dani fighting to gain control over the skittish horse. "What did you do?"

"Nothing. I climbed into the saddle."

"Did I hear you holler?"

"Maybe."

He laughed and rushed forward, grabbing the bit in Daisy's mouth. "Whoa, girl. You startled her, is all. Nice job not falling off." Once the horse had settled down, he stepped back. "Just follow me and the boys. I'll set a slow pace." He climbed onto Lightning, tugged his hat firmly in place on his head, and set off for the woods. The dirt and grass muffled the sound of the hooves as they left the ranch. Birds sang from the trees. The sun hung high overhead, heating his back and shoulders. He glanced over his shoulder at his boys, one on each side of Dani. "Everyone okay?"

"Yes." Dani seemed more relaxed than he'd seen her in the saddle before. She'd be a good rider before she knew it.

The woods greeted him with cool shade. The creek

babbled, inviting them to stop. He pulled on the reins. "Let the horses drink. We'll stop here for a minute, then continue on. I'd like to show you the waterfall."

"You have a waterfall?" Dani's eyes lit up.

"We'll eat there." He took Daisy's reins and led the horses to the creek. A few minutes later, they were back in the saddle and riding through thick brush.

"Wait until you see it," Eric said. "You can stand behind the waterfall. It's so loud you can't hear anything but the water."

"And it's deep enough to swim in," Derrick added. "Dad doesn't let us go that far alone. Not even with Monster."

Speaking of the dog. Monster approached from the right along with Sadie and Heidi. Lightning snorted at sight of the dogs but didn't startle.

When the sound of the waterfall reached his ears, he prodded his horse to pick up the pace. The waterfall had to be his favorite place on the ranch, and he was glad to share it with Dani. Lauren would've loved the spot that seemed cut off from the rest of the world. He slid from the saddle and let the reins drag. The horses wouldn't wander far.

Dani slid from Daisy. "Wow." She stepped to the water's edge. "It's beautiful."

Water fell forty feet from where the mountain rose to the sky and plunged into a swimming hole so deep and cold Dylan had yet to reach the bottom. "Tastes like what I'd expect water from heaven to taste like. I think the source of the creek springs from underground somewhere farther up the mountain."

She dipped her hand in the water. "It's cold."

"It'll turn your lips blue swimming in it." He took

her hand. "Come on. Boys, stay close."

He led her over rocks until they reached the waterfall. Mist coated their skin as they stepped behind the curtain into a small alcove.

"Do animals live in this cave?" She stared wide-eyed around them. "Seems too chilly." She rubbed her hands over her arms.

"Are you cold? We can head back down."

"No. Not yet." She stuck a hand under the water. "Powerful. Have you ever jumped from here?" She stepped forward.

"No." He pulled her back. "You'd break some bones when you hit the surface for sure."

She peered around the curtain and waved to the boys. "I bet you come here a lot."

"Every chance I get." Dylan smiled at the look of rapture on her face as she turned from the water back to the cave.

"Who else knows about this place?"

"Only me, the boys, and now you as far as I know." He leaned against the damp dirt wall. "I haven't shown the men. If any of them found it, they've not said anything."

"It would be a great place to hide." She turned back to the water. "No one would find you here."

He studied her profile, wanting to erase the worry he saw. Hopefully he wouldn't ever need a place to hide. She hadn't mentioned any more text messages, which led him to hope the one sending them had given up.

Buster patrolled the perimeter of the ranch every day, along with one or two of the ranch hands. No one had discovered any new tracks.

"Are you going to bring the campers here?"

"No. This is a special place. There's another waterfall I'll show them."

She turned and smiled. "Good. Too many people knowing would destroy the magic."

Magic. He liked that. Dylan reached for her, wanting very much to kiss her. She must have seen his intention because her eyes widened. Her lips parted. When she didn't step back, he put his hands on her hips and pulled her forward. He lowered his head.

Frantic barking from below broke the spell.

Chapter Twelve

Dani woke before even Mrs. White the next morning and stood at her bedroom window, her gaze on the woods in the distance. The sun barely peeked over the top of the trees.

Her mind dwelled on the kiss that hadn't happened the day before. The kiss interrupted by the barking of dogs at a squirrel chattering at them from a tree. Had she wanted Dylan to kiss her? Yes, she believed so. It had been far too long since a man had looked at her as something to be desired.

A movement near one of the outbuildings had her pressing closer to the window. When the figure of a man stayed to the shadows, she determined it wasn't one of the cowboys. Well, he wouldn't get near the house or the boys' room again.

She slipped her feet into the slippers near the bed and rushed from her room and down the stairs before she could change her mind. From a barrel near the front door, she grabbed an umbrella as a weapon. The old-fashioned pointy end would be better than her bare hands.

On the back deck, she glanced around for the dogs, hoping they could provide backup and scare away the intruder before her bravery fled. The dogs were nowhere to be found and Clarence hadn't been let out of the barn yet. What kind of security were they?

She cast a glance upward toward Dylan's bedroom window. Not seeing any movement there, she leaped off the deck and set off in the direction she'd seen the intruder. Heart beating like a galloping steed, slippers flapping and threatening to fall off, Dani stopped at the barn. She plastered her back against the painted wood and fought to control her breathing.

Common sense flooded in. What exactly did she actually think would happen if she confronted the man? That he would kindly go away and leave her alone? Not likely. This early in the morning, they might be the only two people awake on the ranch.

She frowned. No, there was always supposed to be someone patrolling the grounds. That was most likely who she'd spotted. Embarrassment heated her face. Wait until Dylan heard about this. Hopefully, he'd be more amused than mad.

Convinced she'd overreacted, she stepped around the corner of the barn in time to see someone disappear around the opposite corner. Dani followed, then froze as her gaze fell to a shoe imprint. Not a cowboy boot. A gym shoe.

Her breath fled her body, and she pressed against the building. She hadn't imagined an intruder. Where was the cowboy assigned patrol duty for that hour of the morning? Had something happened to him? She needed to let Dylan know.

She couldn't. If she headed back to the house, she'd be in plain sight of whoever skulked around. No, she needed to keep following him. Eventually, someone else would see and come help her. If she didn't lose the man, they could catch him and hand him over to the sheriff.

Staying close to the building, she peered around the opposite corner in time to see the man duck under the corral fence and head toward the woods. He glanced over his shoulder, his baseball cap pulled too low for her to see his face and sent her tighter against the building.

She gripped the umbrella like a baseball bat and followed, using hay bales and farm equipment—anything she could as cover in order not to be seen. Once he moved past the bunkhouse, there was no way she could follow him without him seeing her. Not until he reached the tree line. Then, she'd have to move quickly in order to catch him.

Where were the dogs? Fear lodged in her throat. The boys would be devastated if something happened to them. The man wouldn't have harmed an animal, would he? If he had, then nothing would stop him from hurting a human in order to get what he wanted.

She glanced back at the house. Still not seeing signs of anyone walking around, she turned back to the stranger. The moment he stepped into the shadows of the forest, she dashed across the wide-open expanse of the ranch in pursuit.

The sun had yet to penetrate the early morning of the woods. She paused to let her eyes adjust and to listen for human sounds that didn't belong. The forest remained silent. No birds sang their morning song, startled to silence by someone trespassing their space.

After a few tense seconds, a squirrel chattered. A bird twittered.

Dani took a deep breath and headed deeper into the woods and tried to catch a glimpse of the man who had drawn her from her room so early in the morning. A twig snapped ahead of her. She froze and ducked.

~

Dylan almost dropped his cup of coffee in the sink when he spotted Dani, dressed in shorts a spaghetti-strap top, and slippers, race across the property and into the woods. He didn't hesitate long. "Mrs. White, watch over the boys." He grabbed the rifle he kept inside the pantry and barged out the back door, the screen door slamming behind him.

Why wasn't the donkey in the corral? Where were the dogs? An uneasy feeling settled in his gut. Something had gone terribly wrong before daybreak.

Shiloh Sloan, one of his ranch hands, stumbled toward the main house. "Someone cold-cocked me, Boss. Hit me from behind with a shovel."

"Have Mrs. White tend to your head and find someone to locate the dogs. I'll check on you when I return. Have someone call the sheriff."

"Where you headed?"

"After Dani." He had a sinking feeling about what he'd find in the woods.

"I'll rouse the guys before seeing Mrs. White." He changed direction for the bunkhouse, holding a bandanna to his bleeding head.

Dylan sprinted for the trees. What was the crazy woman thinking heading out on her own? Didn't she care about the danger to herself? He wanted to wring her pretty neck. Yesterday, he'd wanted to kiss her pretty neck.

The sun peeked through tree branches and dappled

the path with bits of gold light. Dylan studied the ground around him to determine which way Dani had gone. He needed to catch up to her before she caught up to whoever it was she chased.

Since he knew the woods as well as he knew the cleared land in front of it, he didn't doubt he'd find her. The question was in what condition?

He'd pause every few yards or so to listen and study for tracks. All he found was dried pine needles moved aside, a broken twig or two—nothing to show her exact location. He turned toward the creek. Seemed everyone and everything that entered the woods ended up at the creek eventually.

Dani was no different. He found her with her feet in the water and leaning back on her hands as if she hadn't just scared the dickens out of him.

He tapped her on the shoulder.

She grabbed a nearby umbrella, jumped to her feet, and whipped around.

He shot out a hand to keep from getting whacked in the head and yanked the weapon from her hand. "Explain yourself."

She squared her shoulders and took a deep breath. "I saw someone sneaking around the ranch. When I figured out that it wasn't one of the cowboys, I gave chase in hopes someone would come after us in time to catch the guy." She narrowed her eyes. "You didn't come in time."

"Seriously? Do you realize how foolish that was?"

"I wasn't going to let him get close to the house. Not with everyone sleeping. I didn't catch him, I lost my slippers, stepped on a thorn, and stopped to soak my aching feet before heading back." Her eyes flashed.

"What were you going to do if you caught up with him?"

She glanced at the umbrella. "Just keep him under surveillance."

At least she hadn't intended to confront the man. "Come on." He turned to go.

"Who was supposed to be patrolling?"

"Shiloh. He was caught unaware and hit with a shovel."

"Clarence?"

"In the barn for some reason. The donkey doesn't belong in the barn." He suspected the boys were behind that mess-up.

"The dogs?"

"Haven't found them yet." He kept his pace slow because of her bare feet. "Shiloh is calling the sheriff. Hopefully, he'll be here by the time we return. You can tell him your story and let him yell at you. I'm tired of trying to make you see reason. Maybe you'll listen to him."

"I would rather put myself in danger than someone else," she said softly. "This is all because of my choices, no one else's."

He stopped and faced her, putting his hands on her shoulders. "You made some mistakes. Those are in the past. This man is coming on my ranch. That makes this my problem. You don't have to do this alone, Dani. Let me help you."

Her bright eyes clashed with his. "What if you die?"

"I won't."

"You don't know that. What if the boys are harmed?"

"They won't be."

"How. Do. You. Know?"

He lowered his voice. "Because it's you he's after, and that scares me to death."

"Boss." Willy, a pistol in one hand, headed down the path with Buster. "Found the dogs. They'd been given a treat with a sleeping agent, we think. They'll be fine. Did you find the guy?"

"No." He stepped back from Dani. "The sheriff here?"

"Should be soon." Buster glanced from him to Dani, then to her bare feet and pulled a pair of slippers from the back of his waistband. "Lose these?"

"Thank you. They made it hard to run."

He stared at her as if she'd sprouted horns, then shook his head. "Woman, you beat all. You've got the whole ranch on edge." He marched back down the path toward the ranch.

"Guess everyone is mad at me, but I don't care." Dani slid her feet into the slippers. "I did what I thought needed doing."

Nothing he could say would change her mind that she didn't have to do this alone. She'd put herself in the midst of danger to keep him and his boys safe. Why wouldn't she let him do the same?

Gripping the umbrella handle hard enough to snap it in two, he picked up the pace toward home. Let Sheriff Westbrook handle Danica Cooper.

The sheriff waited in the kitchen, cup of coffee on the table in front of him and glanced up when they entered. "Have a seat, Miss Cooper."

She shot Dylan an alarmed look, then sat. "I'd like to get dressed before being interrogated."

"You should've thought of that before chasing after someone threatening you." Sheriff Westbrook wrapped his hands around his cup. "Start from the beginning."

She told him the same story she'd told Dylan, and the sheriff responded in the same way.

"Not the smartest move, Miss Cooper."

"It's not like the man is going to shoot me. He won't get his money if I'm dead." She crossed her arms.

He narrowed his eyes. "You aren't planning on luring him out, are you?" He leaned across the table. "Because I'll lock you up. You and whoever is dumb enough to help you." He shot a look at Marilyn.

Marilyn widened her eyes and put a hand over her heart. "I would never—"

"Right." He planted his hands flat on the table and pushed to his feet. "I'm serious, ladies. Leave it up to me and my deputies to catch this guy."

"You're doing a fine job so far," Dani muttered.

He slammed his hand on the table, causing her to jump. "Going after this man will get you, and most likely someone else, killed. I will not let that happen. This is your only warning, Miss Cooper." He grabbed his hat from the table, jammed it on his head, and marched from the house.

"Well." Marilyn huffed. "There went any plans we wanted to make."

Dylan snapped his mouth shut. They'd intended to try and catch the man themselves? What next?

Chapter Thirteen

He sat at a corner table in the diner and tried to be as inconspicuous as possible. With a tattered baseball cap and denim overalls, he fit right in with all the other hillbillies and country folk. He hoped. The hardest part was speaking with a slight Southern accent rather than a New York one.

Yesterday had been a close call. He'd gotten rid of the dogs and the cowboy, temporarily at least, but he hadn't expected Dani Cooper to give chase.

He stared into his coffee mug. His plan on scoping out the security measures had been successful. There was no way he would be able to nab Dani from the ranch itself. Hopefully, she'd come up with the money he wanted. If not, he'd immerse himself right into the thick of things and take her at the first opportunity.

"Refill?"

He stared up into the face so identical to the woman who had turned his life upside down. "Sure, thanks." It'd be easy to nab her and hold her for ransom, but then he'd have a deputy to deal with. There were enough risks involved without dealing with in-laws.

Dani's twin filled his cup, smiled, and moved on to

another table as the cowboys from the Rocking W ranch, along with Dani and the two boys, crowded into the diner. The owner, Lucy, immediately hustled to clear enough tables for the crowd as if they were royalty.

He ducked his head and avoided eye contact. Hunching his shoulders to hide his body shape, he cut quick glances toward the group. It wouldn't do for Dani to recognize his body shape. When the time came to get close to her, he'd wear some padding. It wouldn't do to raise her suspicions.

Hiding a grin, he sent her a text.

Tick Tock. Time is running out.

It wasn't often he could watch her reaction upon reading one.

She pulled her phone from the back pocket of her jeans and glanced at the screen. Her head jerked up, then she slid the phone back into her pocket, shaking her head when Dylan Wyatt said something.

It took all his willpower not to laugh out loud and give himself away. Toying with the woman between now and when he made his move would be fun. He sent another text letting her know she had one week to get his money, tossed the amount needed to pay for his breakfast on the table, plus a tip, and sauntered from the diner.

~

A week? The menu in her hand shook. She set the menu on the table and glanced at the board displaying the day's special.

"You okay?" Dylan asked for the second time since she'd received the texts.

"Yes."

He leaned closer, his lips to her ear. "You lying?"

She shivered as his breath tickled the hair on her neck. "I'll tell you later."

"Have it your way." He straightened. "With Mrs. White under the weather, it's nice to get into town. The boys reminded me that I don't take them out enough."

"You should do better." She read the special again and decided on the BLT with fries.

Dylan continued to carry on small talk, no doubt trying to take her mind off her troubles. It didn't work. She had one week. One. And her mother and she couldn't leave a trap for the man without running the risk of being arrested and locked up themselves. She had no alternative but let the man come for her. Not even her mother could collect one-hundred-thousand dollars in time, and as everyone knew, Marilyn Cooper could accomplish most things.

Delly stopped at the table to take her order. "You sick?"

"No, why?" Dani frowned.

"You look sick." She shrugged. "What will you have?"

"The BLT and fries. Toasted bread, please." She handed her sister the menu.

Delly studied her face for a minute, then turned to Dylan. "Something's wrong with her. She's either sick or scared. What happened?"

"Today or yesterday? I'll have the mushroom Swiss burger."

"Lordy. Trouble both days?" She shook her head. "I'll never survive this. Never mind. I don't want to know." She continued around the table.

So much for Dani's brave, always-get-things-done

sister. Most likely, her deputy husband had forbidden her from getting involved. Being in the honeymoon stage would be the only reason Delly would be so compliant. Dani wasn't the only stubborn twin.

Dani excused herself and headed for the bathroom. If she didn't corral her emotions, Dylan would demand to know what bothered her. She didn't want to ruin his afternoon on one of the few days the ranch wasn't swarming with guests, and they were all able to leave.

Inside, she splashed her face with cold water, then stared at her reflection in the mirror. She did look ill. Pale and pasty. Worry lined her face, and fear shadowed her eyes. Get a grip! The sheriff would find the man haunting her. He'd never failed before. Why should he now that Dani was in trouble…again? The men of this town trusted the sheriff's department to do its job. So would she. Plus, she was surrounded by cowboys willing to do anything to keep her safe. One in particular. She prayed Dylan didn't come to regret his chivalry. Composure regained, she returned to the table. Her lunch sat waiting for her. Dani's stomach growled. "I guess I'm hungrier than I thought."

"Feeling better?' Dylan smiled and lifted his burger to his mouth.

"I will once I eat." Let him think she was simply hungry. It would save him from asking a lot of questions.

"Want to take a walk later? Just the two of us?"

She paused in lifting her sandwich. "Am I in trouble?"

He chuckled. "No, I thought it would be nice, just the two of us. Get to know each other a little better. Give me a chance to apologize for being heavy-handed in the woods yesterday.”

“Okay.” Wow. Did this mean Dylan was interested in her as more than a nanny for his boys? How did she feel about that? She wanted commitment, a relationship, a family someday, but now when her life was in danger was not the time. Or maybe it was. Maybe she should grab happiness when she could and not wait for a future that might not come. “Sure. I’d like that very much.” She smiled and bit into her sandwich.

~

By the time the sun set, and the twins were in front of the TV watching their favorite show before bed, Dylan was more than ready to spend some alone time with Dani. The surprise on her face when he’d asked was humorous. He had the impression not many people asked to be alone with her.

Dani didn’t seem to have friends in Misty Hollow. At least none that called or came visiting. Her entire world seemed to be his ranch. He wanted her to be happy here.

“Ready?” He passed through the kitchen where she folded dish towels at the table while her mother wiped the counter. “Mrs. White doing better?”

“Just a cold.” Marilyn turned. “Where are you two off to?”

“A short walk around the ranch.” He motioned his head toward the door.

Dani handed the stack of towels to her mother. “I’m ready.”

Her eyebrows raised, Marilyn smiled. “Have fun,” she sang.

Dani rolled her eyes. “It’s just a walk, Mom.” She rushed out the door.

"I might have started some speculation." Dylan caught up with her.

"Yep. She'll rush to tell Mrs. White, who will then let all the cowboys and everyone in five states know." She laughed. "Can you handle it? I mean…I'm Danica Cooper. Bad news."

"You aren't so bad."

"Really?" Her eyes shone in the moonlight. "What have you done in comparison?"

"I killed someone."

She halted. "Okay, you win."

"It was self-defense, but it still messed me up pretty bad. I was at a party with my buddies, smiled at a pretty girl, not knowing she was taken. The boyfriend took offense and came at me with a broken beer bottle. I shoved him, he fell, and struck his head on the side of the house. He died from a brain hemorrhage." That night still gave him nightmares.

"Did your wife know?"

"Yep, and she married me anyway. Lauren is the main reason I got over that night. She helped chase away my demons. It's because of her I have this ranch. Hiring wounded veterans, whether physically or mentally, was her idea."

"She sounds like a wonderful woman."

"She was." He leaned on the paddock and reached out to pet Clarence.

"I wonder how she'd feel about you hiring me as nanny to her sons." She folded her arms on the top rail.

"She'd have insisted." He turned and leaned sideways to face her. "I don't regret hiring you, Dani. Not for a minute. The boys like you. They haven't liked any of their nannies before."

"Hmm."

"What?"

"Nothing." She sighed. "I received another text today at the diner. He gave me a week to come up with the money."

His heart dropped. "What are you going to do?"

She shrugged. "Not much I can do. Mom has thirty thousand she collected as a down payment for Roberto, but that's a far cry from a hundred."

"I'll mortgage the ranch." The words blurted from his mouth so fast they surprised him.

She shook her head hard enough for hair to fall from the hair clip holding the strands back from her face. "You know as well as I do that giving into these demands will have the man coming back for more and more until—" She took a deep breath. "It won't end well, is all."

"We need to let the sheriff know. He has friends in the FBI. They deal with this sort of thing all the time."

The moonlight shone on the tears coursing down her cheeks. "I can't believe you offered to mortgage your ranch for me."

"I'd do anything to put a stop to this." He brushed her tears away with his fingers. "The man is close. Too close." He had to admit she was right. The chances of him stopping at one hundred thousand was slim.

"Mom and I want to set a trap."

"No."

"Listen." She put her hands on his shoulders. "What if the FBI agrees? I could be the bait, then they could pounce and come to the rescue like knights in shining armor?"

He wanted to be her knight. "How can you make

light of this?"

"It beats walking around under a dark cloud all the time." She stepped away. "I promise not to explore the idea any further unless law enforcement agrees with me."

Dylan had no choice but to go along with the idea. He had no claims on her. "I don't have to like it."

"No. Neither do I. Why did you want to take a walk, Dylan? To ask me what my plans are?"

"No. I've been trying to do something for two days." He moved closer.

"What?"

"This." He cupped her head in his hands and claimed her lips. Softly, then increasing the pressure when she kissed him back.

Kissing her might start a fire he wasn't ready for, but he was willing to take the chance of getting burned.

Chapter Fourteen

Dani once again sat in front of Sheriff Westbrook, only this time they were in a conference room rather than in his office. A whiteboard stood at one end of the room. Ten chairs circled an oval table. If not for Dylan's reassuring presence at her side, she'd have fled after seeing a photo of herself on that whiteboard.

Dylan took her hand in his under the table and gave it a gentle squeeze. "It'll be okay."

"The FBI should be here any minute. Can I bring you a soda, water, coffee?" The sheriff hung his hat on a hook near the door.

"No, thank you." Dani wouldn't be able to drink anything without choking.

They waited another half an hour before the feds arrived, agents she recognized from the trouble before. Agents Snowe and Larson sat across from them, moving the sheriff to the end of the table.

"We've heard the case from Sheriff Westbrook," Snowe said, "but we'd like to hear it from you, Miss Cooper."

Dani repeated the texts and the times the man had come onto the ranch, not leaving out her giving chase.

She swallowed against a dry throat. "I think I need to offer myself as bait."

The agent seemed amused. "While that often works, it's a bit early for such drastic measures. We've just arrived. Let us do our job. What we need you to do is stay on the ranch, keep people around you, and don't go chasing after potential suspects. Can you do that?"

She frowned at the patronizing tone and pushed to her feet. "Yes. Are we done here?"

"For now." Agent Larson glanced at Dylan. "When is the overnight camping trip?

"Friday and Saturday night."

"We'll make sure to have someone undercover."

"Will I know who they are?" Dylan stood and put his hand on Dani's back.

"It's best you don't. Just know we'll be there." The agent pushed to his feet and strode from the room.

Dani and Dylan followed. In his truck, she clicked her seatbelt into place. "I guess I understand the need for secrecy, but without knowing who the undercover agent is, we don't know who to trust."

"We don't trust anyone but those employed by the ranch." He turned the key in the ignition, then backed from the parking spot. "I wish I could cancel this camping trip, but it's too short of notice."

The upcoming trip filled her with dread. Most nights, she dreamed of a myriad of things that could go wrong, beginning with and ending with her assailant catching and killing her. It was a good thing she didn't believe that nightmares came true.

"Let's get back and rescue your mother from the boys." He flashed her a grin.

"I'm sure they're baking cookies. Even those two

will behave for cookies." She smiled back, then turned her attention out the window. Acting as if everything was fine grew harder every day. "Do you realize the deadline for me to have the money is Friday? The first night of camping?" She turned back to Dylan. "What if I carry a bag that looks like it might have money in it?"

"You think he'll show up at camp?"

She nodded. "It's the perfect opportunity. Everyone will be too busy to pay any one person much attention. I won't be going anywhere alone, not even to the bathroom, but he'll be there." Waiting for the right time to confront her.

Dylan drummed his fingers on the steering wheel. "I have a military duffel bag that might work."

"You're on board with the idea?"

"Why not?" He shrugged. "You won't be alone. If we act secretive, overly protective of that bag, we might buy you some time. The danger should be low with Buster, the undercover agent, and several of the ranch hands nearby. It won't be easy for him to get to you."

She wanted him to promise she'd be okay. That no one would be harmed, but, no one could guarantee such a thing. All any of them could do was to keep vigilant. Soon, the man would make his move, and this nightmare would be over.

~

Dylan kept an eye on Dani as she trotted the perimeter of the corral on the back of Daisy. The next time she neared the gate, he opened it and stepped back. "Let her have her head. See how you do with her running." He slapped the horse on the rump.

Dani yelped as the mare shot away from the enclosure.

"Don't go too far! Circle the barn."

He laughed as she shrieked again. She'd become adept at riding the horse at a walk, and he wanted to see how she'd do at a gallop. Dani started off bouncing around in the saddle, but she seemed to get the hang of the ride by the third lap.

When she finished, she rode Daisy into the corral, slid from the saddle, and marched up to Dylan. Her eyes flashed. "That was mean. I could've fallen off and been killed."

His blood chilled. She was right. While he'd meant to be playful, he could've caused disastrous results. The image of Lauren lying at her horse's feet flashed through his mind. "I'm sorry. It was time for you to pick up the pace, and I didn't think any further than that."

Her gaze softened, and she cupped his face. "I know. You were playing, and I'm fine. I overreacted. If I wasn't always on edge, I wouldn't have said a thing."

Leaning his forehead against hers, he whispered, "I could've lost you because of goofing around."

"Now I know where the boys get their prank mentality from." She grinned.

He chuckled, loving that she didn't hold a grudge against his stupidity. His teasing could've resulted in something horrible. "Let me put the horse away, and I'll see you back at the house."

"Okay." She stared into his eyes for another second before heading for the back door.

Dylan mentally kicked himself all the way to the barn. "Daisy, girl, I'm a fool." He lifted the saddle from her back. He'd done the same thing to Lauren many times. It had become a game to them, surprising each other, but they were both good riders. If a snake hadn't startled Lauren's horse, she'd still be here. He couldn't expect Dani to step into his wife's spot.

He grabbed the curry brush and let the motion of brushing Daisy's hair soothe away his guilt. Second thoughts about a possible future with Dani ran through his mind. Would he compare her to Lauren? The two couldn't be more different. Lauren's hair had been almost jet black; Dani's a pale blond. Lauren had been almost as tall as he; Dani barely reached his shoulder. One had grown up on the ranch; the other in the big city. It wouldn't be fair to do the same things with Dani that he had with Lauren.

Had he let the danger to her and the ranch cloud his judgment? Was he ready to fill the vacancy Lauren's death left? Now, he wasn't so sure. His heart couldn't take losing another love. He couldn't do it to his boys either. They were quickly growing very fond of Dani. Too fond. They'd all forgotten her role was strictly as a nanny.

The horse taken care of, he exited the barn and closed the door. He took a cursory glance around the area. Clarence grazed where he should be. The three dogs lay on the back deck. Bill Washington, one of his newer hires, patrolled the perimeter. Everything appeared as it should.

Through the kitchen window, his two boys sat at the kitchen table dipping cookies into glasses of milk. Dani glanced up from washing dishes and smiled at him through the glass. He smiled back, but he didn't go inside. Dylan wasn't quite ready to face her yet. There were some things to straighten out in his mind first. He plopped onto one of the deck chairs, his hand falling to stroke Monster's ears. "I'm a mess, ole boy. A real mess."

The dog's only answer was a lick.

"You've got it made, boy. All you have to worry about is when your next meal is. No financial troubles, no romance woes, no worries about when the next danger will strike."

It had been a beautiful early summer day when Lauren died. The two of them had managed to sneak away for a couple of hours without the boys. They had planned a picnic by the creek, but they never made it that far. Sometimes, the best days turned out to be the worst.

He raised a hand to wave at Bill.

~

The man he watched took his second lap around the perimeter. He had no intention of stepping far from the protection of the trees, but he wanted those on the ranch to know how easily he could get to any of them if he wanted to. He gripped the knife in his hand.

There'd be one bang of a surprise soon. One he'd set up days ago. Right now, he had a message to leave—the first of many as the countdown to Dani's deadline loomed.

The cowboy turned slightly, hand raised to his boss on the deck.

The messenger stepped forward.

A twig snapped.

The dogs on the deck sprang to attention and started to bark.

The cowboy spun around, eyes wide.

He plunged the knife into his gut, his heart, then sliced his throat. When the cowboy fell, the other lifted his bloody knife in a toast to the man on the deck, then melted into the trees.

Let the dogs come. By now, he knew his way around the mountain enough to leave them behind. He splashed his way up the creek to erase his scent. The light of the moon guided him as effectively as a flashlight.

Once he'd reached a far enough distance away, he pulled the detonation device from his pocket and pushed the red button. Message number two.

Chapter Fifteen

Dylan leaped from the deck. "Call 911! Find Buster."

A loud pop sounded to his left.

Flames licked at the window of the barn.

Dylan changed direction and rang the bell usually reserved for calling the hands to meals. He kept ringing until his men poured from the bunkhouse. The women spilled onto the deck.

"Get buckets and blankets." Dylan dashed toward the fire. He had to get the horses out. Bill? He faltered, torn between horses and human. His shoulders sagged.

"What is it?" Buster joined him.

"Bill was attacked at the edge of the trees. I saw it. He may be dead."

"Go get the horses. I'll see to Bill." The man pulled his gun from its holster and sprinted in the direction Dylan pointed.

Shiloh already had the barn door open by the time Dylan reached it. "I'll get Daisy; you get Lightning."

"Thanks." The men knew how much he loved that horse.

Lightning reared and neighed, kicking at his stall. Dylan tossed a horse blanket over the animal's eyes, then quickly put a lead rope on. "Come on, boy. It'll be okay."

"What can I do?" Dani hugged a blanket to her chest.

"Wet that and start beating at the flames. Don't get hurt." He tugged his horse until it followed. Outside, he handed the lead to one of his men and went inside to rescue another.

By the time the horses were rescued, the flames had reached the roof, fed by the hay piled along the walls. He grabbed Dani and pulled her back. "It's no use. The barn is a goner."

"Did you get all the animals out?"

"Yes. Where are my boys?"

"Watching from the deck. I threatened their lives if they moved."

He glanced over to see them leaning on the porch railing. His heart rate slowed a tad knowing they were out of harm's way. "Stay close to the house. I need to check on Bill."

"I saw Buster carrying him to the bunkhouse."

He gave her hand a squeeze, then darted in that direction, trusting his men to keep the flames from spreading to any of the other buildings. He felt as stretched as a rubber band over a large watermelon, ready to snap at any minute.

What if he lost everything? The life of his hands? The house? The ranch?

He burst into the bunkhouse as sirens wailed in the distance. Too late to save the barn, but some of the fear choking him dissipated knowing the fire department could save the rest. "How is he?" He knew the answer the moment his gaze landed on the slit in the man's dark throat. Rage replaced fear as his chilled blood started to boil.

"Sorry, Dylan. He was gone by the time I got to him." He covered the ranch hand with a sheet. "I couldn't leave him there, despite it being a crime scene. I'll deal with the sheriff's wrath when he arrives."

Nodding, Dylan turned and hurried from the building. The roof to the barn collapsed in on itself with a groan. The ground shook under his feet. He glanced to the place he'd seen Bill murdered. Everything in him wanted to give chase. To demand answers. Why his ranch hand? The man had done nothing to deserve death.

Spotting the sheriff speaking with the fire chief, he headed that way. "Bill Washington was murdered less than a minute before the explosion that set the barn on fire."

"Explosion?" The fire chief glanced to where his men doused the barn with water.

"I heard a distinct pop. Nothing big enough to blow the walls down, but the fire was definitely set." He went on to explain witnessing Bill's murder. "There was nothing I could do."

"No word from the man responsible?" The sheriff removed his hat and headed for the bunkhouse.

Without him saying so, Dylan knew he was to follow. "Not yet. Unless Dani has heard something, but she hasn't said."

"Where is Miss Cooper?"

Dylan scanned the area, spotting her and the boys near the corral feeding the horses carrots. "She's fine.

Want me to ask her if she's received a text?"

"In a bit." He entered the bunkhouse, shooting Buster a sharp look. "You know better than to remove a body."

"Yes, sir, but these cowboys have a code. No man left behind. Arrest me." Buster crossed his arms.

"Don't tempt me. I need to see where he was killed."

Buster stood from where he sat in a worn, leather chair. "Me or the boss?"

"Dylan. He saw it happen. You stay here and make sure Mr. Washington is taken care of by the medics." Outside, Sheriff Westbrook replaced his hat on his head, muttering something about folks who thought they were above the law.

They trudged across the property until they reached the spot directly across from the back deck. "I had a clear view. The man wanted me to see him." Dylan stared at the blood-soaked ground. "On Bill's second pass, the man stepped out. Bill turned. The man stabbed him multiple times, slit his throat, then waved the knife at me before retreating into the shadows." Was he watching them now?

"The dogs?"

Good question. "They took off after him. I haven't seen them since."

The sheriff glanced at the house. "The security cameras are too far away to pick up the man's face. He's taunting us. We're no closer to finding out who he is than we were on day one. He could be anyone."

Dylan told him about his and Dani's plan to act as if they had the money during the camping trip. "Hopefully, we'll catch him when he goes to grab the bag."

"You could be getting yourselves killed, but I don't have a better idea. Buster will be there, plus our undercover guy. How many ranch hands?"

"Two, and we'll all be armed."

"How many guests?"

"Seven. Four men and three women."

"Add in the FBI agent. That makes five men. Keep Miss Cooper as far away from them as possible."

~

He'd wanted to stay and watch the chaos he'd created, but the dogs had been relentless. Despite his running through the creek, they'd been on his tail all the way to his truck.

Now, he washed the cowboy's blood from his hands, watching the water turn red and run down the drain of his rented motel room. He'd rarely killed, only twice before, and now he wondered—why not more? It had been exhilarating!

He seriously doubted Dani would come up with his money, so the opportunity to kill again would soon present itself. But who? A member of her family? Someone to torment her while she tried to come up with the impossible?

He could head back to New York, gather a few of Robertos men he still trusted, and start building his empire that way, but this way was a lot more fun.

He dried his hands and sent Dani a text, then turned on the television. Soon, the news would run a story about the fire at the ranch. He wanted to watch his handiwork.

Stretched out on top of the bed's covers, he crossed his feet at the ankles and waited to be entertained.

~

"Miss Cooper?"

Dani turned to face Dylan and the sheriff. "Yes?"

"A word please." He motioned for her to step away from the boys.

"I'll watch them." Her mother approached and took her place.

Dani glanced at Dylan, and he nodded. Soot covered his face and arms. Grief shadowed his eyes. She followed them a few feet away from the corral.

"Have you received another text?" The sheriff asked.

She patted her pockets. "Oh. My phone is in the house. When I spotted the fire, I rushed outside without grabbing it. Hold on." She darted into the house and snatched it from the kitchen counter where she'd set it before doing dishes.

"I'll be bringing out coffee and sandwiches in a minute," Mrs. White told her. "The men and first responders will be hungry."

"You're a saint." She flashed a grin and lit up her phone screen. Her smile quickly faded.

The fun has just begun.

"What is it?" Mrs. White glanced over Dani's shoulder. "Fun, is it? What else happened out there?"

"I don't know, but the sheriff and Dylan are very bothered." She took a deep breath and headed back outside where she handed her phone to the sheriff. "What happened other than the fire?"

The men exchanged a glance.

"I have a right to know, same as anyone else on this ranch." She planted her fists on her hips. "This is all because I'm here."

Sheriff Westbrook gave a long exhale out his nose. "Bill Washington was murdered right before the barn caught fire. Dylan saw it happen."

"Oh, no." Tears sprang to her eyes. "I'm so sorry." She'd liked the gentle-spoken cowboy. "This isn't the end, is it?"

"The camping trip is in two days. It'll be over then."

"What if someone else is killed?"

"The men will patrol in pairs from now on. There they are." Dylan bent over as the three dogs stopped next to them. "Where have the three of you been?"

"They're wet, so my guess is they lost the perp in the creek." The sheriff shook his head. "I'll need you to come to the station tomorrow, Dylan, for a formal accounting of what you saw." Shoulders slumped, the sheriff trudged to his car.

"That man is carrying the weight of the world." Dylan sighed. "Makes me nervous. Like maybe he doesn't believe he'll catch this guy."

"We can't think that way. If we do, we've lost." Dani clutched his arm. "Bill won't be the only catastrophe. We have to stay positive."

"It's hard when friends are dying, and everything you've worked for is lying in ashes at your feet."

"The barn can be rebuilt," she said. But Bill would never again draw a breath.

The paramedics passed with a sheet-covered body on a gurney.

She gripped Dylan's hand, giving him whatever support she could. Again, the thought of leaving overtook her. If she hadn't come to the Rocking W, Bill would be alive. The barn would still be standing.

She glanced at Dylan's strong profile. She hadn't know what she'd be missing, this man and his boys. Their lives would have gone on without the jeopardy she'd brought with her. Unknowingly, but still, tonight's events laid solely on her shoulders.

They had to catch this guy. He had to pay. She'd see to it personally.

Steel formed in her backbone, in the set of her jaw. Seeing Mrs. White carrying a tray with coffee and sandwiches from the house, she pulled her hand free of Dylan's. No more showing him how much she cared for him. From now on, she'd keep her distance. Growing close to him would only put him and his boys in harm's way. She took the tray from Mrs. White. "Let me carry this to the men."

"We'll set up a table." She left Dani holding the tray, returning a few minutes later with one of the cowhands carrying a folding card table. "Put that right there, and let the others know about the coffee and food."

"Yes, ma'am." He tipped the brim of his hat and went to spread the word.

"This wasn't your fault, Dani." Mrs. White said as she set the things on the table.

"Trouble followed me here."

"True, but that wasn't your fault. The one responsible for Bill's death s at fault. He made the choice to commit a heinous crime."

"Because of a choice I made months ago." Tears spilled from her eyes.

"If you were my daughter, I'd paddle you." Her eyes sparked. "You cannot take the responsibility of someone else's actions on your shoulders. Its weight will crush you. Chin up and figure out how to stop this man."

Oh, she intended to.

Chapter Sixteen

Dani helped Mrs. White and her mother count the supplies for the third time before they pronounced everything ready. Outside, cowboys milled in preparation for the arrival of those who had signed up for the camping trip—one of whom was most likely the man after Dani, and she had no idea which one. Secrecy was the best chance of catching the guy.

She eyed the army-green duffel bag next to the supplies. By stashing it there, ready to grab as everything else was loaded into saddlebags, she hoped to flee without her mother or Mrs. White asking too many questions.

"We're ready." Eric and Derrick streaked past, tossing their backpacks on the pile with the rest of the supplies.

"Hold on." She grabbed the nearest twin. "Derrick, you and your brother will be carrying your own backpacks. Open them up and let me see that you packed what I told you to." She peered into each bag. "No toys." She pulled out a baseball glove and ball. "Where are your knives? If you catch fish, I'm not cleaning them. You are. Change of clothes?" She pulled out a sheet of paper containing the list of things she'd told them to pack. "Go try again."

Groans filled the kitchen as they took their packs back to their rooms, grumbling about missing all the fun outside.

"If you'd done it last night like I said, you'd be out there with the men right now." She shook her head and slid the duffel next to the supplies when Willy joined them in the kitchen.

He frowned at the stack. "That's all supposed to fit on the horses? This is a camping trip, ladies, not a vacation in Hawaii."

"Food, sleeping bags, dishes…" Mrs. White glared back. "Everything on Dylan's list. If you ain't happy, take it up with him."

"Bossy old woman." He scooped some bags into his arms.

"Cantankerous old man." She held the door open for him.

The bickering between the two almost made Dani forget the danger this camping trip promised. "I'll help you, Willy." She grabbed a bag in each hand, making sure one of them was the duffel bag, and scooted outside before her mother noticed it had been added to the pile.

"Dani." Her mother followed her outside. "Make sure you come home, okay?" Her eyes shimmered.

She dropped the bags she held and stepped into her mother's embrace. "I will. Cowboys are looking after me. You're the one who told me they always save the day." She stepped back and forced a smile. "I promise not to do anything foolish."

"That'll be a first." She gave a shaky laugh.

For once, Dani didn't take offense. Her mother

worried about her and didn't mean anything malicious with her comment. Dani gave her a quick hug. "I'll come in to say goodbye before we leave."

"No goodbyes." Her mother spun around and went back in the house, closing the screen door softly behind her.

"I promised your mother I'd bring you back."

Dani turned and peered into Dylan's face. "She'll hold you to it."

"I know." He picked up the bags she'd dropped. "Tell the boys we leave in thirty minutes. You okay?"

She nodded. "The end of this nightmare is in sight."

"That it is." He smiled and headed to where a line of horses waited for both riders and supplies.

From the front of the house, Buster led the campers to the back deck where he asked them all to wait. "We'll be heading out soon. Toss your packs on the steps. We'll take care of them."

"We're here." The twins barged from the house, packs on their backs, and thundered down the stairs toward the horses. The twins were the only children on this trip. The rest were married couples or single men. Even without other children to play with, there was no way they'd stay behind.

Dani studied the faces of the single men—all in their late thirties to forty, all wearing jeans that looked as if they'd just been bought. Tee-shirts and flannels. Baseball caps. They all appeared excited to be there. None looked like a killer or wannabe crime boss.

She sighed and went back inside for more supplies. Her mother sat at the table, cup of coffee in hand.

"I should be going with you. In fact, I intend to."

Her chin lifted. "I know how to ride. I can do the cooking. Tell Dylan." She bolted up and rushed to her room, calling over her shoulder, "Don't leave without me."

Dani glanced at Mrs. White. "What does she think she can do?"

"Protect her child." She gave a lopsided grin. "Most mothers would do the same. Go on now. Let Dylan know he needs to saddle another horse. Willy will be glad to be relieved of cooking duty."

Did her mother even know how to cook over an open fire? Dani grabbed two more bags and headed outside.

"My mother has decided to come along as cook." She added the bags to the diminishing pile. "She could pose a problem."

"Shiloh, saddle another horse. A tame one." He tightened the cinch on a saddle. "I'm surprised it took her this long to decide. We'll deal with her if she tries to be a hero." His gaze swept over the guests. "Any of them give you a bad feeling?"

"No. At least not yet."

"Keep your wits about you."

"I will." Dani glanced to where the twins already sat in their saddles, wishing she felt the same excitement to head out that they did. She cast another look at the guests before retrieving the last of the bags from the kitchen.

Mom bustled past her with a backpack of her own. "Think I have what I need. I took a peek at the list you gave the boys. And, I have my gun. You?"

Dani nodded. Lord help them all. "Try not to shoot anyone."

"Not unless they come after me or mine." She rushed outside.

Dani hurried after her, relieved to see her mother climbing onto a saddle rather than checking over the supplies. The green duffel bag hung from the saddlebag of Dani's horse, Daisy. If her mother knew it contained a bit of money, just enough to fool someone even temporarily, she'd insist on being part of the plan to catch the man. Dani didn't want to put anyone else in harm's way. Dylan was enough.

~

Dylan glanced at the charred remains of his barn. The structure had been less than a year old. Yes, insurance would pay for a new one, but that big red barn had been a symbol of success—a promise that his ranch would succeed.

He turned as Dani led Daisy to the mounting stump and climbed into the saddle. She'd come a long way in her riding lessons. The camping trip would show just how far. The green duffel taunted him from her saddlebags. Would anyone believe it held a hundred-thousand dollars?

"Ready, Boss?" Willy rode up next to him.

"Yep." He swung onto the back of Lightning. "You mind bringing up the rear?"

"Not at all." He steered the horse to the back of the line while Dylan headed for the front. He'd put Dani and the boys right behind him in case of trouble. Marilyn pulled in behind them. With a flick of the reins, he led the line across the meadow and down the path through the woods.

They'd ride for a couple of hours before stopping to take a break, then a few more hours before reaching the clearing he'd chosen to camp. He'd thought about the waterfall he'd taken Dani to, but he wanted to keep that for the two of them. If too many people knew about the place, they'd hike there. Over time, folks would ruin it, private land or not.

The soft thud of the horses' hooves behind lulled him into a semblance of peace. The sun flickered through the tree branches overhead. A squirrel complained as they passed. Occasionally, soft conversation drifted from behind him. The three dogs wove in and out of the trees like wraiths, noses to the ground.

Still, lingering at the edge of his mind was the worry of where the trouble would come from. Was the man who sought Dani one of the guests, or did he lie in wait, hiding in the shadows of the woods for his chance to pounce? Would the trouble come in the light of day or the dark of night?

Dylan studied the thick brush on each side of the trail as if expecting to see the evil before it struck. He glanced over his shoulder. The twins grinned and waved. Dani looked from one side of the trail to the other, same as Willy and River. The guests chatted, oblivious to the evil that lurked close. Marilyn stared straight ahead, her expression stony.

When they reached the place to take a break, he slid from the back of his horse. "Thirty minutes, folks. Take your relief in the trees. We have sandwiches and water." He moved to help Dani from her horse. "Don't go to the restroom without your mother. Even better, all the women should go together."

"Okay. I'll let everyone know." She stared into his eyes. "It's going to be okay." Her shaky voice belied her words.

"Yep." He forced a smile. "Go on, now. Your mother will need help handing out the sandwiches." Dylan gave her a quick kiss. When all this was over, he planned on asking her if she'd consider a future between them. Right now, until he knew whether they'd to see tomorrow, he couldn't entertain the idea no matter how much he wanted to. Not yet.

While they ate, most sitting on the ground, some leaning against trees, Dylan watched the men. Which one was the undercover agent? The group laughed and joked; some complained about sore rearends. No one seemed overly interested in Dani or the green duffel bag. Of course, no one could tell the bag held money—all that he had from the safe in his office, which wasn't but a couple of thousand dollars—but a quick glance inside might be enough to fool people.

At the end of the half hour, he called for everyone to mount up and went to help Dani. He cupped his hands to give her a boost.

"I really need to learn to do this myself." She put her foot in the stirrup. With a grunt, she pushed and swung her right leg over the saddle, then grinned down at him. "I'm getting stronger."

"You'll be a regular cowgirl before long." He patted her thigh, then went to see if anyone else needed help. Soon, they headed down the trail again.

The hours passed with no surprises. Maybe this camping trip would end without incident. Trouble could come from another direction—a time when they least expected it. It would have to come soon because tonight was the deadline.

~

Oh, what fun it was to pretend. To joke and laugh with the idiots thinking horseback riding and camping were fun. What a lark to act like one of them, all the while keeping his eye on Dani.

He kept stealing glances at the duffel bag, the one thing that looked a bit out of place. Why did she need a backpack and a duffel bag? One of them had to contain his money.

Excitement leaped at the same time as a touch of sadness. How could he keep the fun going after getting his money? Keep asking for more? Maybe, but staying here wouldn't get his empire built. He had to go back to New York for that.

When the trail widened enough, he sidled his horse up next to Dani. "Hello. I'm Steven Langello. Do you work on the ranch or are you a guest?" He saw no reason not to give her his real name. She had no way of knowing his connection to the Roberto family. After all, his relationship with the crime princess had been very hush-hush.

She smiled. "I'm the nanny to those two rascals. Since they insisted on joining this camping trip, I had to come, too."

"Not much of the horseback-type of gal?"

"I'm getting there. You?"

"Born and bred in St. Louis." He did his best to drop the New York accent and add a bit of a twang. "Went to college in California. Haven't had much of an opportunity for this outdoorsy stuff."

"I hope you're enjoying yourself."

"Oh, I am." He grinned. "Things will only get better, don't you think?"

"If you like sleeping in a tent." She chuckled.

"And bugs. There will be bugs."

"Got some spray in my pack. Nice talking to you." He fell back. Side-by-side and she didn't know he was the one who would change her life.

Chapter Seventeen

By the time they stopped for the night beside a mountain lake, every single man in the group had spent time talking to Dani. Not that she minded the attention, what woman would? But, she had her eye on one man in particular. A man she intended to share her feelings with once the danger was past them.

As the men had spoken to her, she tried to get a feel for…something. Not one of them rubbed her the wrong way or caused the hair on her arms to stand at attention. If her radar wasn't working, how could she see the danger coming?

"Pay attention, Dani. I can't put the tent up myself." Her mother handed her a pole. "Slide that through the center, then together we lift. When this is finished, I have to start cooking. If no one catches any fish, we'll be eating burgers and fried potatoes."

"Sorry." Dani followed instructions until they had the two-man tent up and staked to the ground. She eyed the flimsy structure. It would be a tight fit. Dani glanced toward the lake where those who had already put up their tents were trying their luck at catching a fish. The surface of the water sparkled in the late afternoon sun. A fish jumped a few yards from shore, showing promise of a successful catch.

"It's beautiful here," her mom said.

"It sure is. Willy said half the lake belongs to Dylan, the other half to the state. Tomorrow night, we'll camp on government land." If the next stop was as gorgeous as the first, Dani didn't care where they camped. "Boys, let me spray you before you head for the water." She snatched Eric before he dashed past. "You'll be eaten up by bugs if I don't."

"Can you hurry?" He frowned. "All the fish will be gone."

"They will not. Hold still. You, too, Derrick." She covered the boys with the spray, then turned the can on herself. Once she had unrolled sleeping bags in not only her tent, but also in the boys' as well, she grabbed one of the fishing poles leaning against a tree and headed for the lake.

Dylan smiled her way. "Fish much?"

"Whenever we'd visit Misty Hollow when I was a kid. Mostly just Misty Lake, but I've caught a few." She tilted her head. "I can bait my own hook and skin my own fish, although I really hate that part."

"I'll skin any you catch." His grin widened. "You do realize there's a prize for whoever catches the largest fish and another for whoever catches the most, right?"

"I did not." She tilted her head. "It doesn't seem fair that you're fishing."

"Mine don't count." He laughed and cast his line. "You seemed popular during the ride today."

"Yeah, I thought the man after the money would be sure to talk to me, but then they all did. None of them gave me the heebie-jeebies." She cast, her lure landing almost as far as his. "Maybe he isn't here."

"Maybe. Where's the bag?"

"Stuffed in my sleeping bag. It's the safest place I could think of. Since today is the deadline, he's bound to make contact." She glanced over her shoulder to see Buster talking to her mom. "When did he get here?"

"Just now, I guess. He had some things he wanted to finish at the ranch before joining us. I'm glad he made it. We might need him."

Seeing the retired cop who now played cowboy made her more nervous. What if the man who wanted the money knew Buster used to be a cop? He might not make a move, then this whole nightmare would continue. She wanted it all to be over.

"Now, there are four of us to take turns guarding tonight. Got one." He reeled in a largemouth bass that had to weigh a couple of pounds.

"We're going to need more than that for supper." She caught one a bit smaller, but down the lake a short distance, one of the guys got a nice-sized one. The man named Steven, she thought he'd said.

Laughter and good-natured ribbing ensued as the contest went into full swing. The atmosphere didn't lend itself to anything evil. Just a group of people having fun and enjoying each other's company. She strung her fish on the line Dylan provided before casting again.

By suppertime, the group had caught enough fish to feed them all. A woman caught the biggest for a prize of thirty dollars. One of the single men won twenty for the most fish. Dani clapped along with everyone else before joining her mother and Buster by the cookfire.

"I have no idea how to cook fish over an open fire. Or the potatoes." Her mother shot Dani a wide-eyed look.

"I'll help you." Buster pulled flour and eggs from one of the supply boxes. "It isn't hard, just hotter than the average stove. Why don't you cut up the potatoes while I bread the fish?"

Mom immediately calmed. "You are the sweetest man, Buster Jones."

Dani rolled her eyes when her mother batted her eyelashes. She actually batted her eyelashes. Shaking her head, she went in search of the boys. She found them playing in the lake, splashing each other at the water's edge. "Come on. Dry off before we eat, and please don't play in the water without an adult nearby."

"I bet we swim better than you." Derrick darted past her.

Most likely they did. She followed them back to camp, making sure they headed for their tent, then waited outside so they couldn't run off again. Every day she saw why Dylan needed a nanny—even more so on this trip. Bedtime wouldn't come soon enough.

Dylan smiled her way while talking to a married couple. She waved, admiring how easily he seemed to make others feel at home. She was quickly getting to the point where she needed some alone time. If not for the dark cloud of danger looming over her head, she'd scoot into the trees and find a quiet place. Not even her tent would provide solitude, not since she would be sharing it with her mother. Maybe she could find a place on the outskirts of camp. A spot where Dylan and Buster could see her, but where she could be alone for a few minutes.

"Time to eat!" Her mother clanged a metal cup with a spoon.

The guests lined up, plates in hand. Dani stepped to the back of the line with the twins. Once she had her food, she found that quiet spot near her tent and sat on a three-legged stool.

As the group enjoyed the surprisingly good food, the sun set over the mountain. The only light came from the stars and the glow of the fire. Conversations lowered. A bullfrog croaked from the lake. Dani closed her eyes and soaked in the peace.

"Get up nice and slow. Act like everything is fine and dandy."

Her eyes popped open as something hard poked her in the back.

"Do as I say, or I shoot your mother first, then the cowboy you're always gazing at. Then, I'll go to the diner and kill your sister."

Dani pushed to her feet.

"Now, you're going to go get my money. If you alert anyone, I'll shoot. Once you have the money, you're going to stroll real nice around the tent where I'll be waiting. Nod if you understand."

She nodded and slipped into the tent. Her heart beat in her throat. Surely someone would glance her way. Dylan or Buster or one of the other cowboys. She'd set her plate near her stool. More than likely, they'd think she went to the bathroom. If this man took her, how long before they started looking for her?

Her hand sweated around the handle of the duffel bag. Until he counted the money and realized most of it was plain copy paper, she would most likely live. But then…she didn't want to think past that point.

"Hurry up," he hissed from the back of the tent.

Taking a deep breath, she stepped from the tent. The others joked and laughed around the fire. Dylan shot her a quick glance, then turned back to Buster. He hadn't noticed the bag she held behind her back.

She quickly ducked around the tent and came face-to-face with Steven Langello. "You."

"That's right. Now, keep the tent between us and the others and head for the trees."

"Here's the money. Take it and go. I won't say anything for an hour or so." She swallowed past a dry throat. "It won't take long for me to be missed."

"That's why you'd better start walking at a fast clip." He aimed the gun at her head. "*Capisce*?"

She exhaled heavily and headed for the trees.

"Dani!"

Her heart dropped as the twins raced toward her.

"Where ya going?" Eric glanced from her to Steven.

"For a hike, boys." Steven gave a thin-lipped smile. "Come with us."

"Leave them alone."

"No, I think it's best they come with us. What about it, boys?"

"Sure." They scampered ahead of Dani.

"You don't need them." She glared over her shoulder.

"Sure, I do. Wyatt won't try anything if I have his children. Don't worry. I don't hurt kids." He prodded her along with the gun.

"Where are we going?"

"There's a mining road. My truck's there. Once we get there, I'll let the boys go, but you'll be going with me until I know I have my money."

"How far is it?"

"About an hour's hike, if you move it."

One hour. Such a short time for her to devise a plan to save herself and the boys. She didn't know the area well enough to know which way to run if she could get them away. They'd traveled so far from the ranch she doubted even the boys would know. Running aimlessly through the woods would get them all killed. She stumbled and almost fell, dropping the bag.

Steven bent and picked it up. "If you sprain an ankle and can't walk, I'll shoot you and leave you to die on this path."

"You're mean!" Derrick crossed his arms and glared.

"Is that a real gun?" Eric asked. "Why are you pointing it at Dani?"

"No more talking. Keep going."

"My dad is going to punch you in the throat." Derrick turned and stomped down the path.

Steven laughed. "I'm sure he'd like to."

Spotting something in the leaves, Dani scooped it into her hand while Steven kept his gaze on the twins. The plastic key card to the local motel. She slipped it into her pocket. It might come in handy if she got away.

Head high, shoulders straight, she followed the boys in the direction Steven told them to go. On the outside, she might seem compliant, but on the inside, a fire burned, and her mind spun as she devised a plan for escape.

Chapter Eighteen

Dylan looked in Dani's tent then the boys'. None of them or the duffel bag were to be found. His heart raced into overtime. "Buster!"

One look at Dylan's face and the older man came running. "What happened?"

"I can't find Dani or the boys anywhere." He went on to explain about the duffel bag. "It's gone, too."

Buster turned to face the guests. "Who else is missing?"

A man around the age of forty approached them. "I'm Agent Sawyer. What's wrong?"

Dylan repeated himself. "There's a man missing. Steven Langello." Oh, God. He'd taken Dani and his sons. His breath caught, and he bent over to try and keep from hyperventilating. After counting to ten, he straightened.

"Where did you see them last?" Sawyer asked.

"I saw Dani by her tent at suppertime." He pointed out her plate sitting on the ground. "The boys around the same time." That had been almost an hour ago. "We have to go." He put two fingers to his lips and gave a shrill whistle. If Monster was anywhere near, he'd come running. The dog would track the boys.

"I don't want the guests worried." Dylan pulled his gun from his waistband and checked the ammo. "Buster, I'd like you to stay here. If anyone questions where I am, I'm scouting tomorrow's campsite." He'd done that days ago, but as an excuse it should work. "Sawyer, you come with me." He'd need law enforcement to keep him from killing the man who took the ones he loved.

"Sure thing. I'll let the other two ranch hands know what's up." Buster hurried away, no doubt wanting to be the one to go with Dylan.

"I'm going now." After grabbing an article of clothing from the boys' tent, he ran for the trees, the agent on his heels.

Langello. How could he not have picked up something to let him know the man was the one they sought? Once he found out there wasn't the requested amount in that bag, Dani's life and possibly the lives of his boys would be over.

Where was Monster? He'd be searching blind without the dog's keen nose. What about the two guard dogs? Had something happened to them?

"Do you know which way to go?" Sawyer moved up next to him.

"Not yet. There's a path of sorts. I'm hoping to see a sign." How could he not have noticed Dani or the boys gone for an hour? Going ahead with the camping trip despite the threatening text messages had been his dumbest idea yet. Langello probably walked right up to her, then forced her away, and he hadn't seen a thing. Some protector he was.

He studied the ground, hope building when he spotted a shoe print the size of one of the twins. A bit further on, some scuffed leaves, a broken branch on a bush. They'd followed the trail for a while, then veered off to the right.

How far could they have gone in an hour? His boys weren't always the most cooperative. Especially if they didn't like the person giving the orders. Unless they felt threatened. Would they do what they were told if they believed Dani's life to be in danger? He hoped so.

Keeping his attention on the ground in front of him, Dylan kept following the path they'd taken. He wanted to pick up his pace, but going faster could cause him to lose the trail. Patience and prayer were what he needed now.

Agent Sawyer remained silent, simply providing the backup Dylan would eventually need. Occasionally, he could hear the clicking of the man's fingers on his cell phone as he texted someone. Hopefully, the sheriff. They might need help bringing Langello in once they caught up to them.

He forced his thoughts to remain positive, to keep the fear at bay. They'd catch up to them in time; they had to. The alternative was too awful to contemplate. He'd lost one woman he'd loved; he refused to lose another.

Since he doubted Langello had allowed them to bring water, Dylan headed toward the nearest water source. The underground spring that fed the mountain lake bubbled up out of the ground a couple of miles away. Past that was the spring near the ranch. The one with the waterfall, but that was even further. Langello wouldn't lead them back to the ranch, would he?

Maybe. He'd left his vehicle there. It wouldn't be too difficult to get past the guards if the man was patient. The drawback would be the distance. No, Langello had to have a closer means of escape.

"There'll be a copter in the air at first light."

Dylan glanced over his shoulder. "That's hours away."

"Can't search in the dark." Sawyer shrugged. "Hopefully, we'll catch up to them long before that. When we do, I let the sheriff know our location, and he sends backup."

Too long. Dylan returned to his tracking.

Clouds drifted across the face of the moon making sight harder. This forest covered a lot of acres. If he lost the trail, he might never pick it up again. He put his fingers to his lips and gave another shrill whistle. Eventually, the dogs would hear. No matter how dark the night, Monster's keen sense of smell could pick up the trail.

The dog loved the twins. It did occur to Dylan that the dog could already be on their trail, thus ignoring his whistle. The thought made him feel marginally better, but he could really use the dog at his side.

When the moon hid, Dylan fished a small flashlight from his pocket. He hadn't wanted to use it—not wanting to risk Langello seeing him—but in order to continue, he needed light.

Hold on, Dani. I'm coming. He checked his cell phone, knowing before it came to life that he had no service. Even technology was letting him down.

~

A whistle sounded in the distance.

Dani stopped, trying to determine where it came from.

"That's Dad!" Eric fist-bumped the sky.

"Keep moving," Langello growled. "I will start shooting. Remember that."

Dani didn't think he'd harm the boys, but he wouldn't have qualms about killing her. "Let's go, boys." It warmed her heart to know Dylan was on their trail. She needed to slow down without their captor shooting her. Glancing upward, she noted clouds filling the sky. Rain. If the clouds released their burden, tracking would be almost impossible. She stepped between the two boys and put a hand on each of their shoulders. "When the time comes, I'm going to tell you to run," she whispered. "Don't hesitate. Just do it."

They nodded.

Derrick peered behind them. "He might shoot you if we aren't here."

"I'll be fine."

"No talking," Langello called out.

"How much farther?" She asked.

"We'll get there when we get there."

Something rustled in the brush, sending her heart into her throat, then a hint of hope arose. A wild animal might frighten Langello into firing his gun and giving away their position. She peered through the shadows, hoping for something small. Did bears wander at night? Mountain lions did, right? She shook her head to shake away the thoughts. No sense in frightening herself more than she already was.

Monster. She spotted the dog under the bush and motioned for him to stay. The sweet thing had most likely been following them the whole time. Did he know a command to attack? No, that might get him shot. How could she distract Langello long enough to send the boys away?

A deep growling came from behind Monster. Dark eyes glittered. The other two guard dogs had come to the rescue.

She gripped the boys' hands. Then, she started screaming for help.

Heidi and Sadie barked and leaped from the bushes.

Langello yelped.

"Run." Dani took off at a run, dragging the boys with her. Soon, she let go of their hands. They kept up with her, Monster right alongside them.

Langello cursed and fired his gun.

She prayed he wouldn't hit one of the dogs and kept running. "Which way, boys?"

"I don't know this area," Eric said. "Monster, home."

The dog leaped in front of them.

Soon, Dani's breath came in gasps. Her thighs muscles screamed. Still, she forced herself to keep going, urging the boys on until she could no longer hear signs of Langello. Even then, she didn't fool herself into believing he wouldn't follow.

"Stop." She leaned against a tree to catch her breath and relieve the ache in her side. "Just for a minute."

The boys stared in the direction they'd come, their chests heaving. Just then, the clouds overhead released a flood with a vengeance. Soon, all four of them were dripping. It would make it harder for Langello to follow them, but also for Dylan. Through the sound of raindrops hitting the ground came the sound of far-off barking, then a yelp.

Tears sprang to her eyes. Langello had fatally

harmed one or both of them.

She pushed away from the tree. "Let's go." She no longer had it in her for a dead run and set off at a fast walk, ducking branches and weaving around bushes as the forest thickened.

Her feet slogged through the mud, her hair obscuring her vision. She swiped away the wet strands and kept going, glancing back to make sure the boys were still with her. They'd ridden the horses all day. Would they reach the ranch by daylight? The ranch hands would save them. She sure couldn't, having left her gun in her backpack at camp. Dani had been so worried about grabbing the duffel bag and getting away from camp before Langello shot someone, she hadn't grabbed it. She sighed and pushed on. "Recognize anything?"

"Not yet," Derrick said. "Don't worry. Monster knows the way."

She was counting on it.

The more the mud caked on her shoes, the heavier her legs got, and the harder it was to keep going. When Monster glanced back and growled, she increased her pace. Langello couldn't be gaining on them, could he?

Fear threatened to choke her until they crossed a creek after what felt like hours of running. She knew this place. "Boys, is this the creek that leads to the waterfall?"

"I think so." Derrick grinned through the downpour. "We can hide there."

"That's my thought." Dani stepped into the creek, surprised at how hard it flowed. "Be careful. It's running fast." She kept up a fast pace, holding on to low-hanging branches as much as possible in order not to be swept away.

At one point, she moved back, letting the boys move ahead of her. If they slipped, she hoped to be able to grab them before they were swept away.

Soon, the roar of the waterfall rose over the sound of the rain. When it came into sight, Dani led the boys from the creek and stared upward. Climbing would be perilous with the weather, but it was the best chance they had of getting away from Langello until daylight. By then, Dylan would have found them.

"Go slow and careful. It's going to be slippery. I'll be right behind you."

"Promise?" Eric glanced back, one foot on a rock.

"Promise."

He nodded and scampered up as if he climbed in the rain every day. Derrick soon followed.

Dani took a deep breath and started up after them. "Hide, Monster. Go lie down." The dog would be a giveaway if Langello caught up to them.

Her foot slipped, eliciting a shriek from her, before she gained her footing again. *Pay attention, Dani. It's a long hard fall down.* She grabbed a protruding tree root and hoisted herself up and behind the waterfall.

Now, they awaited whatever came next.

Chapter Nineteen

The longer the night, the more dread filled Dylan. A gunshot sounded. His heart skipped a beat. A dog yelped. They were close!

He took off at a run, the agent pounding behind him. They burst into a clearing to see Heidi and Sadie staring off down the trail. Heidi licked a wound on her right front leg.

"Let me see, girl." While Agent Sawyer searched the area for Langello, he checked out the flesh wound on the dog. "You'll be okay. Mrs. White will doctor that up for you when we get home." He pulled one of Eric's socks from his pocket and held it under Heidi's nose, then Sadie's. "Seek."

"No sign of the perp." Sawyer nodded at the dog. "She okay?"

"Yeah. He wasn't a good shot." Dylan straightened. "Go, girls. Find Eric."

"Are they search dogs?" The agent frowned.

"I have no idea, but they're all we've got." He followed the dogs into thicker brush.

They lost the trail a few feet in. The rain, just a drizzle now, had obliterated any tracks or scents. His shoulders sagged.

Refusing to give up, he continued to slog through the mud. A bark ahead of them spurred him faster. "Monster!"

The dog burst free of a juniper bush and jumped on Dylan, leaving paw prints on his shirt. "Boy, it is so good to see you. Do you know where the boys are?"

The dog whined, his tail wagging so hard he might fold himself in half. With another bark, he returned all four paws to the ground and spun away.

After half an hour of shoving dripping branches out of his face, Dylan recognized the direction they were headed. The waterfall. He grinned. Smart girl, his Dani. He waved Sawyer onward.

The noise of the waterfall would drown out his words if he called out to her. Instead, he told the agent to wait at the bottom and started the climb upward. When he reached the top, he inched behind the curtain of water.

Dani, eyes closed and head against the rock wall behind her, had an arm draped across each of his sons' shoulders. He'd never seen anything more beautiful. "Dani."

Her eyes popped open. "You came."

"Of course, I did." He fell to his knees beside her and cupped her face. "I'd storm the gates of hell for you and my boys."

"Dad, we're not going to hell!" The boys both leaped on him, knocking him back.

Flat on the damp earth, he wrapped his arms around them, still staring at Dani. "You okay?"

She nodded. "Did you get him?"

"No. He got away. Let me up, boys. We have to take you all home."

"Back to camp?" Derrick's eyes pleaded.

Oh, yeah, he still had camping guests to attend to. "What do you think, Dani?"

"I think that would be okay, don't you?" Dani asked. "Langello will be long gone. I'm sorry, but he took the duffel bag."

"Then, he'll be back." He sighed and pushed to his feet. "Once he realizes not all of the money is there, he'll come back for it. You should head to the ranch where there's more security."

After a few seconds, she nodded. "I'll go back. The boys can go with you. It's not right to take away their fun because of the trouble I brought."

He groaned. "Again, this isn't your fault." He exhaled heavily, wishing he could convince her she wasn't responsible. "The undercover agent is waiting at the bottom of the waterfall. He can take you back. I'll keep the boys."

At the bottom, he wrapped her in a hug. "Dani, I hate letting you out of my sight. I've never been more scared in my life."

"I'll be fine. As you said, the ranch is the safest place. The agent will take me there. Let my mother know I'll see her when y'all return to the ranch." She caressed his cheek and stepped back, transferring her attention to the twins. "Boys, I've never met anyone braver than you. Behave for your daddy." With another glance at Dylan, she followed the agent away from them.

~

Steven hugged his gun hand close to his body. Stupid dog. She'd clamped onto his hand right as he'd squeezed the trigger, causing him only to wound the other one. Then, he'd run to keep from being attacked. Now, his hand bled down the front of his shirt and throbbed like the dickens.

He slid into the driver's seat of his truck and tossed the bag on the other seat. The other rental could stay at the ranch for all he cared. He had his money and would be gone from this hellhole by morning.

Hillbillies were too much trouble. He had no plan on ever returning to Misty Hollow or anywhere close. Steven cursed against the pain in his hand and turned the key he'd left in the ignition. No one stole a vehicle in the middle of nowhere. No one but him, anyway. He pressed the gas pedal. The tires spun in the mud before gaining traction, and he rocketed back down the mountain.

Finally, the motel came into view. He made a detour to a twenty-four-hour convenience store/gas station, purchased what he needed to doctor his hand, then went to his rented room. A hot shower, a hotdog from the store, and the hard mattress all called his name. Unfortunately, Misty Hollow was in a dry county, so he'd have no beer to help dull the pain from the dog's bite.

When he lay down on the mattress, idly flipping through channels on the television before falling asleep, he dreamed of how he could exact revenge on Dani Cooper for all the trouble she'd caused him. His eyes were just drifting shut when his gaze landed on the duffel bag. A smile spread across his face.

Yeah, he'd be back for more money and revenge just as soon as he started building his empire.

~

Mrs. White, a robe tied tightly around her, stared at

Dani and Agent Sawyer from the kitchen door. "I'm guessing there's been some trouble."

"You could say that." Dani grabbed a hand towel and rubbed some of the water from her hair. "It's all good now. I'm going to take a shower. After some sleep, I'll fill you in."

The agent stepped forward. "If it's okay with you, I'll crash on the sofa once my clothes dry. The sheriff will be here later to take your statement."

Now that the adrenaline of fleeing from Langello had ebbed, exhaustion weighed on her. Dani's steps dragged as she made her way to her room.

She undressed, turned the shower as hot as she could stand, then climbed in, lifting her face to the spray. The heat washed away both dirt and the chill that had seeped into her bones from the rain and the waterfall.

How would Dylan explain her absence to the guests? Not only was she missing from the group, but Sawyer and Langello as well. The boys were sure to say something. Would her trouble cause even more problems for the ranch? Guests might feel it was too dangerous to sign up for camping trips on the Rocking W.

Dylan already struggled to keep the ranch on its feet. Now, he'd lost the money from his safe and, possibly, any future income. She could replace the two thousand from the safe, and her mother would help, but she couldn't help with the ranch's future. Not with the danger still out there.

She turned off the shower and wrapped a towel around her hair, then used another one to dry her body before donning an oversized tee shirt to sleep in. She glanced at the clock. One a.m. That was all? The flight through the woods had seemed like an eternity.

After making sure all windows were locked, she did the same with her bedroom door. Langello had managed to sneak onto the ranch before, finding a way past cowboy security. She'd feel safer knowing he couldn't get to her if he stepped foot on the property again.

Dani glanced out the window in the direction of the woods. Dylan and the campers wouldn't return until mid-morning of the next day. Hours of idleness stretched in front of her. When was the last time she could say that? She pulled the curtains closed and picked up her dirty clothes. As she went to toss them into the clothes hamper in her closet, a hotel room key fell out.

Dani picked it up and stared at it for a few seconds. Okay, she now knew how to spend the idle hours until Dylan returned. She would put an end to it all come morning.

Chapter Twenty

After a few hours of sleep, Dani snuck into the kitchen before Mrs. White woke up and took the gun the cook kept in a cookie jar on top of the refrigerator. She left a note where she knew it would be found, but not for a while. After making sure the chamber in the gun was full, she slid the weapon into the waistband of her jeans and darted to her truck.

She had a surprise for Mr. Langello. No more waiting for trouble to come sneaking up on her. This time she would meet it head-on. By the time the sheriff came, everything would be under control.

Drat. She glanced through the rearview mirror as she drove away from the house. The two cowboys on patrol stood staring after her. Dani didn't have as much time as she'd thought. They'd contact Dylan, then the sheriff, and the whole gang would come running to stop her. She had to end it all before the man hurt someone she cared about.

Langello had already said he'd go after her mother, then Delly, before turning to those on the ranch. Had he discovered the shortage of funds?

As she drove, she cast continuous glances in the rearview mirror to make sure no one followed. If they did, she'd have to lose them. She needed time to face Langello, then the calvary could arrive. Once she had the man secured, they could take over, but not before he answered some questions.

~

Fresh from another shower, Steven sat at the small round table in his motel room and unzipped the duffel bag. He grinned at the sight of cash. His smile faded as he lifted out the top bundles to discover plain copy paper underneath. He'd been duped.

He cursed and threw the TV remote across the room. It hit the wall with a thud, leaving a dent in the drywall. Someone in the adjacent room yelled and banged on the wall for him to settle down, or they'd call the manager.

Let them. Steven itched for a fight. His blood boiled. He knocked the blank paper to the floor.

Why hadn't he checked the money when he'd grabbed the bag? All his work…for nothing! So much for heading back to New York.

He lunged to his feet and paced the small room. This was all Danica Cooper's fault, and he'd make her pay. Oh, yes, she would be very sorry very soon—she and her family.

~

Dani parked in front of the hotel and located the door to the manager's office so she could find out which room belonged to Langello. She couldn't very well try every door, could she? There had to be fifty rooms. Dani needed a good story…she smiled and climbed out of the truck.

A bell jingled as she pushed open the front door. A young woman peered up with a smile. "May I help you?"

"I found this outside." She set the card key on the counter. "Also, I'm meeting Steven Langello, and he neglected to tell me which room he's in." She pasted on a smile.

"I can ring him for you."

Dani shook her head and leaned closer as if sharing a secret. "I'm early. It's our anniversary, and I want to surprise him."

"I'm not sure—"

"Oh, come on. Girl to girl. Surely, you understand. My name is Danica if you want to check." *Please don't check.*

"I guess it would be okay." Her fingers flew across the keyboard. "Room 210, second floor. Happy anniversary."

"Thank you." She whirled around and strolled to the elevator. Inside, she pushed the button for the second floor. Her heart rose into her throat as the car lifted.

She patted her pocket for her cell phone, then remembered she'd left it at camp. It didn't matter. They wouldn't need it to track her. She'd said in the note exactly where she was headed minus the room number.

Taking a deep breath, she knocked on room 210, then pulled her gun from her waistband. When the door opened, she aimed the barrel at Langello's head. "Inside and close the door."

His eyes sparked as a grin spread across his face. "The little girl has a backbone."

"Shut up. Sit in that chair." She noticed the bag on the table and the scattered pieces of paper. "Temper tantrum?"

He sat and crossed his arms across his bare chest. "If I'd known I was going to have company, I'd have put on some pants. It's a little cold in my boxers."

"I have some questions I want answered before the sheriff arrives."

He frowned. "Guess you'd better start asking."

"Why me?" She needed to know why he'd come after her. "I don't know you."

"I had a plan." He leaned forward, sitting back when she aimed the gun at his heart. "I was in an affair with Roberto's daughter. We had plans to take over the business."

"She was already in a relationship." Dani had seen her with the man herself.

"Not for long. Why do you think she joined her father in this podunk town? Because she planned to take over, convert his men to her side, and kill the ones who wouldn't join her. But then, you and your family changed all that. I still plan on building an empire. The plans on how have simply changed." He laughed. "I could use a woman like you on my arm. Beautiful, brave, not stupid."

Not being stupid was debatable as the sheriff would tell her when he arrived. Same with Dylan. It shouldn't be long. She'd already been gone an hour.

"I didn't have the money for Roberto. What made you think I could come up with it for you?"

He shrugged. "Desperate people always find a way. Once I started killing your family, you'd find the money, even if you had to steal it."

"You're delusional." She ought to pull the trigger and save the taxpayers money. "I'm a recovering gambling addict who now works as a nanny."

"Who works for a prosperous horse ranch."

"Not yet, it isn't." But, God willing, it would be someday.

He shrugged again. "The man has horses. Good ones. If he needed money bad enough, he could sell them. As I said, there is always a way." He stood and took a step toward her.

"Sit back down or I'll shoot you."

"I don't think you will."

She aimed the gun at his thigh and pulled the trigger.

He cursed and fell to the floor, calling her every bad female word that existed.

Dani tilted her head, her hand shaking. She was as surprised that she'd shot him as he was.

Someone in the room next door pounded on the wall saying they were calling the police. Good. The sheriff should've been here by now anyway.

Dani marched to the bathroom, grabbed a towel hanging there, then returned and tossed it to Langello. "Might want to hold that on the wound so you don't bleed to death."

"You are cold-hearted."

"Why is it that a killer takes it personal when the tables are turned?" She perched on the edge of the bed. "You're right, though. I didn't think I had it in me. But, when those you love are in danger, it's amazing what a person can do. Now, my family is safe, and you're going to prison. Not much you can do about building an empire from there."

~

When Buster informed him about the note Dani had left, Dylan couldn't return to the ranch fast enough.

He'd left the campers in the capable hands of Buster and his ranch hand, saddled Lightning, and rode like the hounds of hell were on his heels.

Back at the ranch, he put the horse still saddled in the paddock and made a beeline for his truck. Sheriff Westbrook had told him he wouldn't wait and intended on heading to the motel without Dylan.

Please, God, let the sheriff have reached there on time.

He must've broken a speed record driving down the mountain. What was Dani thinking going after Langello alone? Why did she insist on doing things herself?

When he arrived at the motel, the sheriff and two other squad cars sat out front, lights flashing. An ambulance idled close by as two paramedics wheeled Langello out on a stretcher.

Shoving open the door to his truck, Dylan scanned the parking lot for Dani. Not seeing her, he raced for the ambulance, expecting to see her injured or dead.

"She's still inside." One of the paramedics motioned his head toward the building. "Second floor, room 210."

When he reached the elevator, the doors opened. Dani and the sheriff stepped out. Dylan wrapped her in a hug. "Woman, you're giving me gray hair." He glanced at the sheriff. "Everything okay?"

The sheriff sighed. "Said she shot the man in self-defense. It's her word against his. Since he's wanted for murder, I'm guessing there might be some truth to her story."

He didn't believe that any more than Dylan did. "Let's go home, Dani. I have some things to tell you."

Keeping his arm around her and giving the sheriff a nod, he led her from the building and out to his truck. Inside, he faced her. "Do you realize I could be crying over your body right now?"

"I had a gun." A slight smile teased at her lips. "Shot him in the leg." She paled and thrust open the truck door before vomiting. Done, she sat back up. "Guess I'm not as tough as I think I am."

He laughed and shook his head. "You're the toughest person I know."

"Are the boys at the ranch?"

"No. They'll be back tomorrow along with everyone else. Today and tonight is for us."

Her eyes widened. "Are you going to fire me?"

"No, I have something else planned." He backed the vehicle from the motel and headed back up the mountain.

When they reached the ranch, he told Mrs. White he didn't want to be disturbed, then led Dani to his office. From the stricken look on the cook's face, she most likely assumed that he did intend to fire her. No, but the office was the one place he knew they wouldn't be disturbed. Inside, he closed the door, then turned to her. "Please sit." He motioned to one of the padded leather chairs.

Dani slowly lowered to the chair and folded her hands in her lap. She took a deep breath and straightened her shoulders. "I'm ready."

He knelt in front of her and took her hands in his. "I love you, Danica. My boys love you." Her hands trembled as tears filled her eyes. "I never thought I'd find another woman I wanted to spend my life with. Not until you walked up the road to my house. When I opened that door and looked into those nervous eyes that morning, I knew there was no way I could let you go."

"I love you, too," she said softly. "That's why I went to Langello. He threatened to kill everyone I love."

"I know." He kissed the top of her hands before meeting her gaze again. "Will you marry me, Dani?"

"On one condition."

"Anything." His heart leaped.

"That it's a small wedding by the waterfall. It's all I want."

"That I can do." He cupped her face and kissed her.

Epilogue

A week later, wearing a simple white gown of satin, Dani strolled down the path toward the waterfall and her new life. Her white cowboy boots, a gift from her sister, crushed the white rose petals littering the path.

The sun kissed the waterfall with diamonds. Standing at the edge of the pool was Dylan, gorgeous in a black suit. No cowboy hat shaded his handsome face.

"We both got ourselves a cowboy," her mother whispered, tightening her arm in Dani's.

"You and Buster?" She arched a brow.

Her mother nodded. "He's wonderful. The Cooper women are lucky indeed."

Dani couldn't agree more. Everything she'd ever dreamed of waited for her just a few feet away. Not only a caring husband, but also two wonderful boys. Her heart raced as she strolled closer.

Smile on his face, eyes lit, Dylan turned to face her as the other cowboys and a few friends from town stood. No church could have been more beautiful than this spot right here. Dylan's private sanctuary he shared with his family and friends…with her. The two of them would spend their honeymoon night behind the curtain of water, shut off from the rest of the world, all the noise of the world pushed away, leaving just the rush of the water.

Dylan said he'd make sure everything was ready, whatever that meant. Her mother released her, then went to stand by Buster.

Dani's gaze locked on Dylan's. There'd been whispers around town that the two of them didn't know each other well enough or long enough to get married. She disagreed. Dani knew everything she needed to about the wonderful man standing in front of her.

Brave, caring, moral…a man who would do anything to protect and provide for his family. A man who had dropped everything to come for her. Yes, she knew all she needed to know about Dylan Wyatt.

The pastor spoke loudly in order to be heard above the roar of the waterfall. When he pronounced them man and wife, and they shared their first kiss as a married couple, Willy led Lightning and Daisy, both with flowers in their manes and tails, to the wedding couple.

Dylan helped Dani onto her horse, gave her another kiss, then climbed into the saddle on Lightning. Cheers and applause rose as they rode back up the path Dani had come down just a short while ago.

"Mrs. Wyatt." Dylan grinned.

"Mr. Wyatt." Dani prayed she never gave him another day of grief. She had jeopardized her cowboy enough for a lifetime. "Let's get this reception over with, so you can show me what's behind waterfall curtain number one."

Later, as the sun kissed the top of Misty Mountain, the two of them climbed to what would be their suite for the night. Plush comforters and pillows spread over a tarp. A bucket of ice held a bottle of Champagne. A picnic basket sat nearby.

Dani smiled and turned, stepping into her husband's arms.

Stay tuned for the second book in the Cowboys of Misty Hollow series, *Cowboy Peril*.

Dear Reader,

I hope you're enjoying this spinoff from The Secrets of Misty Hollow series. It's always fun to return to old friends and meet new ones. And who doesn't love a cowboy?

If you enjoyed this book, please head over to Amazon and leave a review. Spread the word by telling your friends. Reviews and word of mouth are like gold to an author.

God bless,

Cynthia

Did you read the other Misty Hollow books?

Misty Hollow
Secrets of Misty Hollow
Deceptive Peace
Calm Surface
Lightning Never Strikes Twice
Lethal Inheritance
Bitter Isolation
Say I Don't
Christmas Stalker
Bridge to Safety
When Night Falls

A Place to Hide
Mountain Refuge

Stay in Misty Hollow for a while. Get the entire series here!

www.cynthiahickey.com

Cynthia Hickey is a multi-published and best-selling author of cozy mysteries and romantic suspense. She has taught writing at many conferences and small writing retreats. She and her husband run the publishing press, Winged Publications. They live in Arizona and Arkansas, becoming snowbirds with three dogs. They have ten grandchildren who keep them busy and tell everyone they know that "Nana is a writer."

Connect with me on FaceBook
Twitter
Sign up for my newsletter and receive a free short story
www.cynthiahickey.com

Follow me on Amazon
And Bookbub
Shop my bookstore on shopify. For better prices and autographed books.

Enjoy other books by Cynthia Hickey

Misty Hollow
Secrets of Misty Hollow
Deceptive Peace
Calm Surface

Lightning Never Strikes Twice
Lethal Inheritance
Bitter Isolation
Say I Don't
Christmas Stalker
Bridge to Safety
When Night Falls
A Place to Hide
Mountain Refuge

Stay in Misty Hollow for a while. Get the entire series here!

The Seven Deadly Sins series
Deadly Pride
Deadly Covet
Deadly Lust
Deadly Glutton
Deadly Envy
Deadly Sloth
Deadly Anger

The Tail Waggin' Mysteries
Cat-Eyed Witness
The Dog Who Found a Body
Troublesome Twosome
Four-Legged Suspect
Unwanted Christmas Guest
Wedding Day Cat Burglar

Brothers Steele
Sharp as Steele

Carved in Steele
Forged in Steele
Brothers Steele (All three in one)

The Brothers of Copper Pass
Wyatt's Warrant
Dirk's Defense
Stetson's Secret
Houston's Hope
Dallas's Dare
Seth's Sacrifice
Malcolm's Misunderstanding
The Brothers of Copper Pass Boxed Set

Time Travel
The Portal

Tiny House Mysteries
No Small Caper
Caper Goes Missing
Caper Finds a Clue
Caper's Dark Adventure
A Strange Game for Caper
Caper Steals Christmas
Caper Finds a Treasure
Tiny House Mysteries boxed set

Wife for Hire – Private Investigators
Saving Sarah
Lesson for Lacey
Mission for Meghan

Long Way for Lainie
Aimed at Amy
Wife for Hire (all five in one)

A Hollywood Murder
Killer Pose, book 1
Killer Snapshot, book 2
Shoot to Kill, book 3
Kodak Kill Shot, book 4
To Snap a Killer
Hollywood Murder Mysteries

Shady Acres Mysteries
Beware the Orchids, book 1
Path to Nowhere
Poison Foliage
Poinsettia Madness
Deadly Greenhouse Gases
Vine Entrapment
Shady Acres Boxed Set

CLEAN BUT GRITTY Romantic Suspense

Highland Springs

Murder Live
Say Bye to Mommy
To Breathe Again
Highland Springs Murders (all 3 in one)

Colors of Evil Series

Shades of Crimson
Coral Shadows

The Pretty Must Die Series

Ripped in Red, book 1
Pierced in Pink, book 2
Wounded in White, book 3
Worthy, The Complete Story

Lisa Paxton Mystery Series

Eenie Meenie Miny Mo
Jack Be Nimble
Hickory Dickory Dock
Boxed Set

Hearts of Courage
A Heart of Valor
The Game
Suspicious Minds
After the Storm
Local Betrayal
Hearts of Courage Boxed Set

Overcoming Evil series
Mistaken Assassin
Captured Innocence
Mountain of Fear
Exposure at Sea
A Secret to Die for
Collision Course

Romantic Suspense of 5 books in 1

INSPIRATIONAL

Nosy Neighbor Series
Anything For A Mystery, Book 1
A Killer Plot, Book 2
Skin Care Can Be Murder, Book 3
Death By Baking, Book 4
Jogging Is Bad For Your Health, Book 5
Poison Bubbles, Book 6
A Good Party Can Kill You, Book 7
Nosy Neighbor collection

Christmas with Stormi Nelson

The Summer Meadows Series
Fudge-Laced Felonies, Book 1
Candy-Coated Secrets, Book 2
Chocolate-Covered Crime, Book 3
Maui Macadamia Madness, Book 4
All four novels in one collection

The River Valley Mystery Series
Deadly Neighbors, Book 1
Advance Notice, Book 2
The Librarian's Last Chapter, Book 3
All three novels in one collection